MISS SEPTEMBER

MISS SEPTEMBER

A NOVEL

FRANÇOIS GRAVEL

TRANSLATED BY SHEILA FISCHMAN

CORMORANT
BOOKS

Miss Septembre was first published in French by
Éditions Québec/Amérique.

The publisher gratefully acknowledges the support of the Canada
Council for the Arts and the Ontario Arts Council for its publishing
program. The publisher also acknowledges the financial support of
the Government of Canada through the Book Publishing Industry
Development Program for its publishing activities.
The translator gratefully acknowledges the assistance of the
Canada Council for the Arts.

Cover design and imagery by Bill Douglas @ The Bang.

Printed and bound in Canada.

Canadian Cataloguing in Publication Data
Gravel, François
[Miss Septembre. English]
Miss September : a novel
Translation of: Miss Septembre.
ISBN 1-896951-11-2
I. Fischman, Sheila II. Title. III. Title: Miss Septembre. English.
PS8563.R388M5713 1998   C843'.54   C98-900965-3
PQ3919.2.G755M5713 1998

CORMORANT BOOKS INC.
RR 1, Dunvegan, Ontario K0C 1J0

CHAPTER 1

Even though he was only twenty-seven, Detective Lieutenant Brodeur sometimes wondered if his old colleagues were right when they maintained that everything was better *before*, when there were still snowstorms worthy of the name, when the National Hockey League had only six teams, when baseball players were paid reasonable salaries. Before, when women were women and men were men and beer still tasted like beer. Before, when bank robbers used crowbars, picklocks and stethoscopes, not bulldozers and dynamite.

While he couldn't judge the other matters, Brodeur had to admit that, where bank robberies were concerned, his colleagues were right. In the past, bank robbers spent days and nights digging tunnels, which took guts, imagination, nerves of steel, and good team spirit — not to mention a sound knowledge, constantly updated, of alarm systems. That golden age, if it really had existed, had long since ended, and the aristocrats of crime had been recycled into other fields: computers, drugs, prostitution, or politics — areas that were less risky and much more lucrative.

The thieves Brodeur had locked horns with in the course of his young career weren't artists, far from it; they weren't even honest craftsmen; they were just poor jerks who banded together in small groups, shot up whatever was available, and improvised jobs that usually fell apart. If they weren't using bulldozers to smash the walls of the bank so they could get their hands on the automatic teller machines — a lot of trouble for a few thousand dollars — they were using dynamite on the night deposit vaults. The results were equally mediocre: they'd place tons of explosives against the wall of the bank, and their take would be a pile of debris with the night deposit vault lying under it, still intact. More often than not they just left it there, since they weren't strong enough to lift it.

Intelligent bank robberies had become as rare as happy marriages, Brodeur was thinking as he puttered along the highway. A bank heist that was a little masterpiece? Tell me another one! Yet that was how the duty officer who'd wakened him at two a.m. had described it: a little masterpiece of a bank heist.

He'd barely had time to gulp a coffee before pulling on boots and overcoat, rummaging in his pockets for the car key, and charging down the stairs, excited at the prospect of a real investigation to work on. After that he'd raced full tilt down the highway till he skidded on some melting snow. A few centimetres more and he'd have driven smack into the pillar of a viaduct.

That was when he'd slowed down and, to encourage his heart to resume its normal rhythm, tried hard to do nothing but watch the snowflakes falling gently, as if suspended in the night. A masterpiece of a bank heist? Since when did dynamite produce masterpieces? He'd be dealing with another bunch of poor jerks who'd been a little luckier than most, that was all.

Another twenty kilometres. Stuck for something to keep his mind occupied, Brodeur stuck a cassette in the tape deck. Led Zeppelin. "Stairway to Heaven." Suzanne's favourite.... He ejected the cassette, pressing the button so hard he nearly broke it, then threw it outside, hoping a ten-ton truck would run over it. No music. No more music. Nothing but snow and silence.

And what if the old guys were right? Maybe life really was simpler *before*, when everything ran in slow motion. The good Lord must have made a mistake pressing the fast-forward button, so that it jammed.

Give me a nice neat bank robbery, please, something to keep my mind occupied. Give me hundreds of suspects to interrogate, no matter how pathetic. That's one of the great advantages police investigations have over love affairs: the suspects are liars, but you know that in advance.

§

Brodeur had never been in this small village in the Laurentians, which might not be the busiest but was certainly the classiest in the region.

Several vaguely Swiss-looking houses with pointed roofs, exposed beams, and giant fieldstone chimneys were huddled around the small Anglican church, which was no longer used but was still kept up because it was pretty. No vulgar restaurants here, and certainly no seedy motels: discreetly lit signs pointed the way to inns and B&Bs. Everything was so clean and quiet that for a moment Brodeur thought he'd been closed up inside one of those glass balls that fill up with falling snowflakes if you shake them. The comparison wasn't as banal as it seemed; since restaurant-owners decorate their windows with artificial snow, isn't it possible that the owners of ski hills bring out their snow guns at nightfall to keep their village looking like a postcard?

He had to drive another few kilometres before he finally spied, in the middle of nowhere, a small shopping centre that boasted a drugstore, a supermarket, a few clothing and souvenir stores, and, finally, the local branch of the Bank of Montreal, with two patrol cars and an anonymous Jetta parked in front.

The patrolmen, though they were used to making maximum noise under such circumstances, were probably intimidated by the affluent look of the village and hadn't turned on their flashers or sirens. They were simply waiting, sitting quietly in their cars and sharing a thermos of coffee.

Though he was dying to beg a coffee laced with lots of sugar and cream from his colleagues, Brodeur first made his way to the bank. The night deposit vault, obviously. Gutted so neatly that it was as if the robbers had used a can-opener. To get results like that they must have placed the dynamite inside the vault, indicating a certain understanding of explosives, or maybe just plain old intelligence. One or two sticks, no more, had been slipped in through the slot, as easily as a letter into a mailbox. The dynamite lands on the bags of deposits and ka-boom.... No vault could resist pressure like that. The problem was, the canvas bags in which businesses place their take wouldn't have resisted either. What's the good of blowing up a vault if all you get out of it is some charred bills?

"Sandbags."

"What?"

Lost in thought, Brodeur barely noticed the policeman who'd come up to him with a cup of coffee.

"First of all, they slipped dozens and dozens of little sandbags through the slot. The bags fell into the trap, then into the vault. Once the deposits were well protected, they just dropped the dynamite in on top. The sand absorbed the explosion and the bills stayed intact. Not bad, not bad at all."

"What kind of bags?"

"Plastic Ziplocs. Most of them melted in the explosion but there are a few pieces left. There must've been fifty at least, maybe more. Fifty bags of sand dropped in one at a time.... Takes patience."

"What time was it?"

"Couldn't say. Nobody told us. If we hadn't been out on a routine patrol we wouldn't have known till the bank opened. We assume it was sometime between eleven p.m. and two a.m."

"Nobody heard the explosion?"

"No."

"Footsteps in the snow?"

"Nope. All swept up."

"*Swept?*"

"You got it. Maybe with a real broom or maybe with one of those brushes for taking snow off your car windows. The experts should be here any minute, but hopes of finding anything are pretty slim. If they went to the trouble of sweeping up their footprints, we can assume they had the brains not to leave fingerprints."

Brodeur had finished his coffee, eyes still glued to the gutted vault, and his brain immediately resumed its normal operation: the experts wouldn't find anything, the patrolman was right. They'd have to follow their usual *modus operandi*. First, put out a general call in case there had been a similar robbery in the region, which would be very surprising. Then search the memory of G-12, the fantastic computer database that would give him a list of individuals who might have committed such a robbery; he'd have fun with that, checking out every cross-reference imaginable. He had a good idea what he'd turn up, though. Night deposit vaults? A hundred and twelve entries. With dynamite? Sixty. With bags of sand protecting the deposits? Sorry, no entries at all.

So then they'd go back to the good old methods: question the hotel, restaurant, and garage owners in case they'd seen any suspicious customers (skiers without skis, for instance); then study the list of people who were licensed to use dynamite; answer the appeals of the town's leading citizens, who'd want to denounce the local punks, outsiders, and brothers-in-law.... Something told him this was liable to be a long investigation, and he was not at all unhappy at the prospect.

"That guy in the Jetta, who's he?"

"The branch manager. He came as soon as he got word, but of course he didn't see or hear a thing. You want to talk to him?"

The question was pointless; as soon as he'd sensed that he was being observed, the manager had got out of his car and headed for the two cops.

A young man, athletic-looking and amazingly calm, dressed as if for a wedding in an overcoat open to a silk foulard that set off a white shirt. Wakened in the middle of the night, he hadn't had time to tie a necktie, which was comforting to Brodeur, who in his own haste had simply pulled on a pair of jeans.

"Lieutenant Brodeur? Let me introduce myself: Robert Brown, the manager. This is a terrible nuisance, just before Christmas.... What do you think of all this?"

"For the time being, not much — except that it's a fine little robbery."

"A *little* robbery?"

"With the kind of clientele in this village, I imagine they mostly pay with American Express. What would they want with bank statements?"

"You're forgetting the drugstore, the ski hill, the stores, the supermarket.... Have you any idea how much a Provigo takes in on a Thursday five days before Christmas?"

It was as if an electric current had shot between the bank manager, who suddenly become sombre, and Brodeur, whose eyes lit up.

"How much?"

"I'd say at least two hundred thousand."

"In all? I mean, does that include credit card transactions?"

"No, that's just the small bills. And it's not calculating the exchange rate; there are lots of American dollars around."

Two hundred thousand dollars, at least.... A robbery that's not just intelligent but profitable. Enough to keep my mind busy, thank you, Lord.... First of all, find a restaurant;

then start right in on the investigation, while the iron's hot.

After giving some instructions to the men on patrol — don't touch anything till the expert arrives, don't say anything to journalists about the sandbags, string up yellow tape — and promising the manager he'd keep him posted on how the investigation was going, Brodeur took a last look at the front of the bank.

The manager and the four policemen, who had got out of their cars, stood in a semicircle around the vault, erect and solemn. All they needed was a cold rain and some umbrellas and they'd look like a grieving family meditating over a fresh grave. But with those big flakes of luminous snow falling gently onto their shoulders, the scene was more evocative of a gathering of the faithful praying outside a grotto where the Virgin Mary had appeared.

Brodeur felt an urge to thank her; she'd given him a wonderful Christmas present.

Chapter 2

Geneviève Vallières, who for the occasion answered to the name Roxane, had peeled off the white towel from around her neck and slung it over the rack beside the door; next, in a gesture that might suggest a certain hesitation, she'd brought one finger to her mouth, then decided to take off her track suit. It was warm, after all, and she should make herself comfortable. While Percy Sledge was belting out "When a Man Loves a Woman" on the tape deck, she slathered herself from head to toe with almond oil that made her skin glisten and scented the whole room. Then, without much conviction, she launched into a series of warm-up exercises that may have been necessary but still appeared ridiculous in this cramped little room.

While the decor looked just like a gym, complete with foam mat, wall bars, and big mirror, it only took one exercise ball and two small barbells for the room to be crowded; it was hardly bigger than a double bed.

Drops of sweat were mingling with the almond oil now, giving her skin an attractive coppery shimmer, and Geneviève massaged herself very slowly while she got her breath back. The real workout always coincided with the start of her favourite song, "A Whiter Shade of Pale."

She sat cross-legged, holding the little barbells in front of her, first exhaling slowly, then inhaling as she spread her arms as far as possible, as if she wanted to embrace the entire earth. These movements, which acted on the deltoids and the pectorals, had a peculiar effect on her breasts, which stood at attention. Sometimes, when she was in the mood to have some fun, she would execute these movements very quickly, so that her breasts seemed to be vibrating in a way that was irresistibly funny — to her, at any rate. That day, though, she stayed with slow movements, exhaling slowly every time she brought the weights back in front of her, as if to chase away all the ideas that had been cluttering her head ever since she'd come back from what she called euphemistically her "little expedition."

A few hours on the road, an overdose of adrenalin that still wasn't totally eliminated, and the deed had been done; she'd finally got what she needed to live on for a few years without having to rack her brains. She felt absolutely no remorse; the bank she'd robbed could just as well have been destroyed by lightning, in which case thousands of dollars would have vanished to no avail, and the insurance companies would have reimbursed the depositors. An artificial thunderbolt had had the same result, with just a few slight differences: instead of going up in smoke, the banknotes had ended up in her pockets — or rather, in the trunk of her car. What was the problem?

The problem was all these images that were cluttering her head, that she couldn't shake off.

The image of a Honda Civic, lost in the falling snow. The dashboard display showed that she was driving at seventy kilometres an hour, that the engine was turning at 3000 rpm, that the gas tank was full and the engine temperature normal. If Geneviève's body had been attached to instruments like these, she would have read that her pulse was a little faster than usual, that her hands were damp and her throat a little dry, but that overall she wasn't nearly as nervous as she might have thought. How had she been able to stay so calm — she who'd never committed the slightest act of plagiarism at school, or swiped even a lipstick from a drugstore? You can try to anticipate everything but you never know how your body will react; hers, though, had worked wonderfully well. Thank God she hadn't drunk or smoked or snorted anything, preferring to concentrate on taking regular, long, deep breaths, the kind that lower your pulse rate perfectly naturally, down to sixty beats a minute.

The postcard village, where she'd often gone skiing with her parents when she was a child, she had seen now in a new light: a pretty village with just one bank and no sign of a police station.

The deserted parking lot, the trunk, the bags of sand dropped into the narrow slot one at a time. The two sticks of dynamite, surprisingly heavy (Geneviève had always assumed that dynamite would be like giant firecrackers); the long wires, slowly unwound and attached to the nine-volt battery. The detonation. A crackling sound, like an electrical transformer blowing, that had made her jump.

The night deposit bags, still warm, that she'd gathered up one at a time and stowed in her trunk. The brush she'd used to sweep away her footsteps (the thief has very small feet, the police would have said). The Honda that got gallantly back on the road.

The dry throat, the pulse that had shot up to a hundred and forty, which she'd managed to bring down slowly, first to a hundred and twenty and then to a hundred, as if it were adapting itself to the little red arrow on the speedometer. *Slow down, Geneviève, slow down, it would be silly to get yourself arrested for speeding....* Ninety kilometres an hour, eighty beats a minute, eyes that have trouble looking away from the rearview mirror, tension normal, the road is open, the pavement's nearly dry, the mind clear, magnificently clear, don't turn on the radio, nothing but silence.

The body had worked and so had the mind — at least until she closed her apartment door behind her and set down on the kitchen floor a heavy canvas bag, the kind hockey players use.

No sooner had she got to the bathroom than her body

started to tremble, to perspire, to empty itself through all its orifices. Then the mirror sent back to her a stricken face that looked twenty years older. She'd thought it was a portrait of her mother. And then that insidious little voice telling her that it wasn't over, it would never be over, it had barely begun.

The first chords of "Stairway to Heaven" came just in time to drive away these images. Geneviève immediately put down her weights, massaged herself to speed up the circulation, then lay down on her stomach facing her exercise ball. The game consisted of using her forehead to push the ball towards her chin, then towards her abdomen and pelvis, then back to its original position. As well as straining the muscles in her arms, which had to support the weight of her body all this time, the exercise worked wonders on the trapezoids, the dorsals, and the gluteus maximus. Sometimes, to change the routine, she would roll the ball under her pelvis as if to charge it with energy, then project it under her chin with one quick movement. But that day she wasn't in the mood for games. No sooner were her eyes closed than she saw again the canvas bags piled on the kitchen table, which she'd had to open by Caesarean section. The fabric had resisted her scissors but not her knives, which were blunted by the operation. She'd had to dispose of them, along with the disembowelled bags and the credit card statements, in two garbage bags which she'd simply dropped off a few streets away. They would be crushed by the truck before they were incinerated or buried under tons of garbage, and no one, not even the seagulls, would ever track them down.

The take was well beyond her expectations: two hundred and forty-four thousand six hundred and twenty-seven dollars, and that didn't take into account the exchange rate on the thirty-odd thousand American dollars. Enough to make neat stacks of bills that covered the table, which she'd gazed at like a good haul of Hallowe'en candy.

It's too easy, it's too good to be true.... The little voice had made itself heard again, the same little voice that gave her no respite and seeped into all her dreams. Geneviève had wakened in the middle of the night in a sweat, in spite of the sleeping pills she'd popped, and she had to take more long breaths to bring her heartbeat back to normal. It was a nasty little voice that resisted both breathing exercises and logical arguments.... Let's go over it once again, you have to.

Tire marks in the snow? As if there were only one Honda on the road with Michelin tires.... She'd had them changed the next day, in any case.

Someone who might have seen the automobile, an insomniac who spent his nights at the window noting the licence numbers of the cars that drove down the main street of the village, just like that, to amuse himself? The Honda was so dirty he wouldn't have been able to make out the number, or even tell exactly what colour it was. In the winter all Hondas are grey.

The dynamite? Okay, let's study all the hypotheses. Imagine a policeman with incredible foresight, who after a series of totally unbelievable coincidences would trace her back to the bar on Labelle Boulevard where, for the sum of two hundred dollars, she'd obtained the two yellow sticks. We'd also have to suppose that the Hell's Angel was still alive, that he wanted to co-operate with the cops, and that he had a phenomenal memory: "Sure I remember.... Seems to me it was November. This young chick, average height, red hair...." Oh yes, he'd remember the hair: a flaming red wig. Maybe he'd also noticed the beauty mark drawn on her cheek. Unless life resembled a very bad detective novel, you could brush aside that hypothesis.

And the bags of sand, while we're at it? At the first flakes of snow, garage owners sell tons of sand, and there's no law against stuffing it into plastic bags.

An accomplice who'd open his trap one night while he was drinking? What accomplice? Even more than her technical preparation, Geneviève was proud of the fact that she hadn't told anyone her plan, not a single person, which had actually been much harder than she'd imagined. She had often thought about her brother, Louis, who was always inclined to boast about his exploits, real or imaginary, who at twenty-five still collected trophies, real or imaginary. He would never have been able to keep such a secret.

Unless she herself did something foolish (and why would she? She only had to be careful, that was all), no one would ever find her trail. A perfect robbery, with neither witness nor accomplice.

Magical thinking. It only happens to other people. That's what you thought the day Guillaume....

What did Guillaume have to do with it? All right, it's true, math wasn't on our minds that night. We took a chance and I didn't get pregnant. Which proves that it's wrong to condemn magical thinking; it works a lot more often than we think.

The little voice finally fell silent. If logic couldn't solve it, why not turn to bad faith?

Her mind free at last, Geneviève allowed herself to enjoy her workout. She imagined herself stretched out on top of Guillaume, slowly moving her pelvis the way she was moving it on the exercise ball now, savouring every movement; Guillaume had many flaws, but he knew how to give her pleasure, that she had to admit.

"Mademoiselle?"

What does this guy want? The song isn't even over.

"Mademoiselle? Mademoiselle Roxane? You can stop now...."

Geneviève had to shake herself to clear her mind. This was the moment she hated most in her lousy job: the noisy breathing of the client who had watched the show and satisfied himself as best he could, and was now tearing off a paper towel to clean up the damage.

When he got his breath back, he started talking about this and that, as if Roxane were just a hairdresser. His idiotic remarks didn't really hide his shame, but it was still better than the insults she sometimes had to take without a word.

He sits there slumped in his chair, holding the paper towel, his dick already limp.

"I don't know what you were up to today, but it was fantastic.... Worth every penny."

And Geneviève looks at him, incredulous; how can he be satisfied when I didn't even look at him?

"You're so beautiful...."

The usual compliment. Does he really think it makes me happy to hear that? You've paid your fifty bucks, you poor jerk, didn't they tell you the tip was included?

As she gets back into her track suit, Geneviève gives him a smile like the host of a telethon and, to leave him with a happy memory, licks her index finger, rolling her eyes. You have to look after your clientele, especially when they're polite, and it's good exercise for the orbicular and masseter muscles.

Presently, when the client turns his back, she'll do her final exercise: standing in the very centre of the miniature gym, she'll raise her middle finger towards the sky, and it won't be to know which way the wind is blowing.

CHAPTER 3

"You haven't changed your mind? If it's the salary, you know, we can work something out. We think very highly of you...."

"No, that's not it."

"What will you live on?"

"I'll manage. I've been saving."

"If you need a break you could work part-time. It isn't always a barrel of laughs, I know that, but we've always treated you well, haven't we? Elsewhere...."

Geneviève waited, legs chastely crossed, for her boss to finish calculating her hours and sign her final cheque. Each time he completed an addition, he looked at her over his little reading glasses and bombarded her with questions, until she grasped the key word: *elsewhere* it would be worse, *elsewhere* she wouldn't be so well protected, *elsewhere* she'd be at the clients' mercy....

He had got rich off her and all the others by holding on to half of her fees, but in all honesty Geneviève had to admit that her boss had always behaved himself. He respected the girls in his way, didn't even allow himself to use their Christian names. In fact, he barely looked at them; he much preferred the company of his computer, and spent his days with it, walled up inside his office like a good civil servant. During this time the girls put on their show in perfect safety, with no fear of their admirers going too far; the sight of Bob, who cracked his knuckles in the foyer all day long, had a deterrent effect on any clients who might be a little too bold. And they'd have to be very reckless to do anything out of line in a house that, as was common knowledge, belonged to a consortium made up of a dozen former Montreal policemen. Cops enjoyed a reduced rate, which explained why there were always two or three in the waiting-room.

Elsewhere. So that was what he was worried about. She'd have to find a way to convince him that she'd never go to work for the competition. He was still trying to come up with arguments that might keep her on the job when she spied, on a corner of his desk, a colour photo in a gilt frame. A little girl, aged four or five, smiling with all her baby teeth at the Zellers photographer. Then Geneviève bowed her head as if to admit a shameful secret:

"Don't worry, I'll never go to work for another agency. Actually, I don't want to work any more. It's a question of...of religion."

From the silence that greeted this revelation, she guessed that she'd scored a point. Now all she had to do was drive the nail in.

"It's my boyfriend, you see. He's very religious. He wants us to have a church wedding, have children, all that — and he wants me to stay home and look after them."

With her head still lowered (how had she been able to keep a straight face?) she heard an awkward throat-clearing, then the creak of his pen and some crumpling papers. When she looked up again the boss was holding out her final paycheque, stammering congratulations and apologies, obviously embarrassed. It's very easy to turn a man on, thought Geneviève as she stuffed the cheque into her purse, but it's even easier to move him.

§

She wouldn't miss her salary, now that she had other means. She would never think about her clients again, those boastful little businessmen who never shed their cellphones, the timid students who raised their voices when they came in and blushed shyly as soon as her clothes were off, the frustrated husbands who came to brighten up the colours of their fantasies, and the unemployed foremen who were prepared to pay fifty dollars to persuade themselves that they still had power — for half an hour, at any rate. Despise them, said the other girls, get revenge. Geneviève had always had trouble with that; her clients inspired only indifference, pity, disgust, and, occasionally, outbursts of hilarity that were hard to hold back. On what, then, or whom, could she take revenge?

She wouldn't miss her clients, she'd miss her bosses even less, but she would think often about the girls with whom she'd shared so many cigarettes, Diet Cokes, and shreds of confidences when they chatted in what they pompously called their dressing-room, between clients.

Tao, the Cambodian, who played the oriental card with great swoops of her fan, deep bows, and timid smiles but betrayed her integration into Quebec society by cursing like a longshoreman when a client spattered her kimono. Tao, who was thirty-five and looked twelve; Tao, who always dodged any questions about the circumstances that had brought her to Montreal, preferring to tell risqué stories that made them collapse with laughter.

Pamela, the lovely Caribbean (which somehow sounded more erotic than the lovely Haitian), who had to struggle twice as hard as the others for the same salary, and take the worst insults without flinching. *Never mind, I still turn them on, the sons of bitches*, she would repeat to her mirror, as if that represented tremendous power.

Chantal the erotic hairdresser, a genuine hairdresser who plied her scissors while her clients jerked off under their capes. She had to spend a long time in the shower afterwards to get rid of the hair and beard clippings, which itched. If she had a free moment between cuts, she would amuse herself making "transformations": some touches to her makeup, a few strokes of the brush, or a well-chosen wig — that was all it took for Chantal to be transformed into an Arabian dancing girl, a waitress, a schoolmistress, or Ilsa, she-wolf of the SS.

Nancy, who, because of a certain distinguished *je ne sais quoi*, called herself Alexandra; she'd taken Geneviève under her wing when she started out: "Tits they've seen hundreds of, and a lot nicer than yours. You can fondle them all you want, it's the eyes that matter, it's your eyes they look at. They want to see a woman who likes it, know what I mean? And you have to wear perfume. Lots and lots of perfume. See, a page from *Playboy*, a porn video, those don't smell. No makeup, you're right, you're nature girl, but a wig, there's nothing like a wig to make you feel like somebody else."

Danièle, the nurse who spent her time buttoning her tight uniform so she could unbutton it in front of her "patients," and who wouldn't hesitate — for a supplement — to find a very unusual use for what could pass, in a pinch, for a thermometer. Danièle, who never took off her immaculate nurse's cap when she did her act. "It's for the image," she liked to repeat. "Without it they'd forget that I'm a nurse, and then...." Most of the time the phrase stayed in suspense. But the truth, as she confided to Geneviève one day, was that her headdress was the last refuge of her modesty. She could never have put on a show if she had felt truly naked.

Tao, Pamela, Chantal, Nancy, Danièle and the others all had in common the one good reason to be working at Le Pussy: twenty-five dollars a show. At two shows an hour, on a busy night they'd go home exhausted, but ten times richer than if they'd worked themselves to death filing invoices, giving haircuts to customers who'd jerk off under their capes anyway, wiping little old men in nursing homes, or teaching young executives on the make how to firm up their abs.

Tao, Pamela, Chantal.... Girls with a poor self-image, as Geneviève's mother would have said. Losers, as her father would have put it. Yet they were all there, squeezed into the dressing-room, to celebrate the departure of Roxane the gymnast. Let the clients wait ten more minutes, they'll only be more excited.

Each of the girls had come to give Geneviève a kiss on the cheek, and Tao made a presentation on behalf of them all.

"It's for Christmas, we forgot to give it to you then," she said, biting her lips as if she were holding back the giggles.

To draw out the pleasure, the girls had used so many boxes and wasted so much tape that the present was harder to open than a safe. When she finally succeeded, Geneviève discovered, wrapped in tissue paper, a collection of plaster figurines, grossly hand-painted and extremely ugly. Either Taiwan craftsmen are particularly clumsy or they've never seen live models of oxen, asses, sheep, and camels.

When she got the reference, Geneviève finally burst out laughing like the others.

Danièle was the one who had led off one night when they were all exhausted: "I had two asses and an ox today. And did they puff! As if their little Jesus needed warming up...."

Ever since that day, any client with a spectacular physical feature or his own highly personal way of moaning had been given a place in the great family of animals. As well as oxen and asses, their zoo contained a fair number of owls, frogs, fish, snakes, and slugs. And very few stallions.

When she was leaving, Geneviève came very close to sharing a final confidence with them: do what I did, girls. All you need is a few bags of sand and two sticks of dynamite, and you'll be able to take it easy. But no one would have heard her; all the girls were watching Tao and her famous imitation of hippopotamus clients, who spent a long time searching for the little willies under their huge bellies.

She said goodbye to Bob one last time, in the foyer, and she was surprised to see how small he was, nearly frail. "It's not about muscles," he liked to say. "And it's not about karate either, it's about your look. It's all in the eyes, that's where it happens." To prove it, he put on his bodyguard expression, and right away he was fifteen centimetres taller.

After that, Geneviève walked through the door and took a good breath of fresh air. It was over.

§

She'd stayed in her Honda for a few moments, waiting for the engine to warm up and the windows to be de-iced. Barely two minutes. Long enough to spy three clients walking into Le Pussy. The first two affected a casual look while the third, ashamed, was huddled inside his overcoat. He looked like Robert, the most pitiful liar she'd ever met. Robert, who knew how to talk to women and could have as many as he wanted — which didn't stop him from coming to Le Pussy to stroke his trophy. Robert, who had highly placed friends in the police and the underworld, who hung out with cabinet ministers, who knew so many things about them that he could make them quake in their boots if he decided to talk — sure, Robert, but come here and shake your trophy, let's get it over with.

Robert, who always read his *Journal de Montréal* in the waiting-room and had something to say about every one of the crimes: "They set the dynamite against the wall, the idiots. Do that and all you get is, it makes a noise. *Inside* the vault — that's where you have to put it. But I suppose you're wondering what happens to the bills if the vault blows up?"

"Yes, you're right, what does happen to the bills?" Bob had asked wearily.

"Not a thing! You use sand to protect them! It's like shepherd's pie: a layer of deposit bags, a layer of sand, and the dynamite on top, like mashed potatoes. Smart, eh?"

And Robert tapped his forehead to show how brilliant

he was.

And he wasn't crazy, little Robert. Just a bit of a blowhard. The kind of man who talks a lot and whom nobody listens to. You have to be paid, well paid, to put up with a person like that. And why listen to them anyway, when you can simply pretend?

But Geneviève didn't pretend.

§

She drove through the city streets like a zombie, her head churning with images as if they were trying to hollow out a nest for themselves in her memory: the girls from Le Pussy, Bob cracking his knuckles, dynamite, trophies, the plaster animals, little Robert; images that would emerge from their nest at night to remind her that she'd spent six months of her life in that place.

CHAPTER 4

Geneviève opened the door a crack, slipped one arm inside her apartment to reach the switch, then pulled the door all the way open. The living-room was empty and no sound or suspicious movement came from the kitchen or bedroom. She shut the door, fastened the security chain, and resisted the urge to look through the peephole to make sure there was no detective hiding behind a newspaper at the end of the corridor. There wouldn't be one, any more than there'd been a suspicious automobile in her rearview mirror.

She kept her coat on while she took off her boots, and then very slowly opened the bedroom door. The bedspread wasn't rumpled, the wicker chair was still empty. A hundred times she had envisaged a policeman absent-mindedly cleaning his nails. "I've been waiting for you," he'd say without even looking up. Nor was there a man in a raincoat inspecting the toilet tank. Nobody.

Two weeks after her little expedition, she hadn't received even one visit or phone call. Could they have closed the file?

Watch out, Geneviève. Just one indiscretion, one extravagant purchase....

Just one indiscretion? Who could she talk to in this big empty apartment where the only company she had was that little voice of hers? At least it had been behaving itself for a while now. Nearly in league with her, even, as if it had got used to the idea.

Just one extravagant purchase? Not that she hadn't had the urge to act like those lottery winners who blow their bundle on a Jaguar or a dream house. But Geneviève hadn't changed her habits. She'd just treated herself to a few innocent little luxuries, some clothes she'd been wanting for a long time, a few books and records — like a student who'd worked in a camp all summer. She'd paid cash for all her purchases, just as the student most likely would have done. Do the police start an investigation whenever a young woman survives for two weeks without using her credit card?

Geneviève went back to the door, peeled off her coat and scarf, and hung them in the closet, at the same time giving a little kick to the two cardboard boxes at the very back. Two boxes she'd had the bright idea of keeping on the day she moved into this apartment; with a felt pen she'd marked all six sides BOOKS. Judging by the sound, they still contained seventy thousand dollars.

Then, out of habit, she checked the other hiding places. Twenty thousand dollars still at the back of the kitchen cupboards, in cookie bags. In her freezer, carefully wrapped in aluminum foil, she'd managed to fit another twenty thousand.

Happy are those who win the lottery, who can deposit their loot in the bank with impunity and quietly live on the interest. But deposit a quarter of a million in small bills? Before she'd had time to fill out the deposit slip, every cop on the planet would have been notified. She'd also considered opening a dozen accounts in various branches, renting as many safety deposit boxes and stuffing them with bills, but she'd decided against taking such a risk. Who knew whether a message would show up on a computer screen in the office of some Big Brother? *Attention, irrational increase in number of bank accounts and safety deposit boxes. For suspect's Social Insurance Number press F6, for licence number press F7, for tax file press F8, to transmit foregoing information to nearest police station press F9.*

And so, while she waited to come up with something better, she resigned herself to turning her apartment into a bank branch and to sleeping and eating inside a safe. From the kitchen she moved on to the bathroom, where she'd hidden another twenty thousand dollars in a box of tampons; then back to the living-room, where she automatically turned on the television in the vain hope of taking her mind off things. Every break for an earsplitting commercial made her jump, and she turned off the sound whenever she thought she heard a suspicious noise in the corridor. She had so much trouble concentrating that the dumbest cop show seemed incomprehensible, but she sat there anyway, in front of the silent TV set, looking at disconnected images.

A few times she tried to bury herself in a good thick novel, but all she saw was an endless series of black lines filing past, devoid of meaning. When she had still been living with her parents she had spent voluptuous hours lazing in a bubble bath, but now she had trouble staying in the shower for two minutes.

And so she fell back on the TV set and zapped till she found a National Geographic special. As long as she hit the mute button to escape the unctuously preachy ecologists, she managed to relax, sometimes, by watching moonfish dancing, iguanas mating, or lions yawning — all these animals that spent their lives doing nothing. Why couldn't she do the same?

When she'd decided to work for two weeks longer than necessary, Geneviève had wanted to avoid a coincidence that might rouse suspicions. But who could have drawn a connection between a bank robbery and the resignation of a well-bred young woman who, contrary to all expectations, had held out for six long months at Le Pussy?

You were afraid of being idle, that's all.

What would you have done, all alone in your empty apart-

ment? Pace the floor and bite your nails? Build castles with your wads of bills while you waited for the police to smash in the door? The little voice was right, as usual. Geneviève couldn't even allow herself to take the trip she'd dreamed about for so long: to drive across the United States listening to country music, climb the Colorado mountains, watch the sunrise over the Grand Canyon, admire San Francisco Bay, and then slowly make her way back through Vancouver. If a customs officer suffered an attack of zeal and searched her car, such an expedition would probably end at the Vermont border: "Do you really need two hundred thousand dollars in small bills?" And even if she got across the border, how much fun would it be to check in to motels when she couldn't sleep for fear of her car being stolen?

She would never have imagined that it was so hard to do nothing, or so complicated to spend money.

She often thought about those old people who try to give themselves the illusion that their days are full: they go to the store in the morning for their litre of milk, go back an hour later for the paper, then again in the late afternoon for a small bag of sugar — as small as possible, to give them an additional reason to leave their prison once their supplies have run out. Others sign up for recorder, pottery, or oil-painting lessons, visit museums, or sit and gawk at their TV set, watching days and more days go by, all alike, mired in boredom. To spend your whole life working only to end up like that…. But there's worse: to end up like that at the age of twenty-two.

She was doomed to hide her money under her mattress, like a little old lady; to stuff herself with Valium, sleeping pills, and television, like a little old lady; doomed to silence and fear, like a little old lady; doomed to think up tricks to make the time pass, like a little old lady.

A hundred times, when these ideas had crossed her mind, she'd thought of stuffing all the money into the big hockey bag and dragging it to the nearest police station: I found this on the street, I don't know what's in it but there's something fishy about it....

A hundred times, she'd run to the bathroom. Planted in front of the mirror, she ruffled her hair, twisted her mouth, sucked in her cheeks, wrinkled her brow, distorted her face in horrible grimaces so she'd look like the little old lady she had become. And then she'd splash cold water on her face and look again. A few drops of water acted like the most miraculous regenerating cream; her skin, as if by magic, was smooth again, without a trace of wrinkles, and covered in the freckles that made her look even younger than twenty-two. Then she made herself smile, showing her teeth, which were even and wonderfully white, and ran her hands through her hair, which fell gently into place just like a shampoo commercial.

She dabbed some more water on her forehead and cheeks and grew younger by another few years. She was fourteen and spending hours at her mirror, studying everything that didn't suit her: lips that were too thin, a nose that was slightly long, eyes and hair both a very ordinary brown, legs that were too short.... As long as she stayed in the bathroom, she could convince herself, during her worst moments of masochism and negativity, that she was ugly. To persuade herself of the contrary, though, she only had to go outside. While she wasn't the type to attract the first glance, she'd always been able to catch the second. She had never lacked suitors, and she'd often led her teachers on, just for fun. A forthright smile and they'd begin to stammer, an idiotic smile plastered on their faces, and they'd forgive her for any late assignments, accepting her lamest excuses.

Then Geneviève went all the way back to when she was seven; even then she used to study herself in the mirror, desperately looking for a halo ever since her grandmother had told her she looked like the Blessed Virgin.

After that she left the bathroom, pulled on coat and boots, and went for a walk around the neighbourhood, with no precise goal. She walked very quickly, decisively, paying not the slightest attention to passersby or store windows, simply trying to accelerate her heartbeat and fill her lungs with fresh air so that great bursts of oxygenated blood would clear her brain.

Walk very fast, even faster, almost running, and don't think, don't reason, life isn't a math problem, the kind you solve with one two three four fives and small *a*, small *b*, small *c*, regardless of what the teachers may think.

Once upon a time there was a math teacher who'd summoned Geneviève to his office and reprimanded her because her average had dropped from eighty-two to seventy-three: watch out, Geneviève, your future is at stake. She was fifteen then and her entire future was reduced to two little numbers. The next month she'd managed to lower her average to sixty-seven, and at the end of the year she triumphantly reached her goal with a masterly sixty. That's what I think of your future.

Her father, crestfallen, had looked at her report card and talked about the thousands of dollars he'd had to shell out for her private school, about the sacrifices he'd had to make in order for her to succeed. A highly rated school, with teachers who still know how to teach spelling — that's what you need to be a winner. And piano lessons, there's nothing like music to teach you what hard work and discipline are all about.... Performance, again and always.

The week after that, she gave up the piano. She had never known what she really wanted, but she did know that she wasn't going to collect any trophies.

She'd attended university just long enough to collect a diploma, the least impressive one possible. Her phys ed degree had enabled her to land her first job, in a fitness centre catering to businessmen. She was paid seven dollars an hour to encourage them to firm up their abs by pedalling machines that measured pulse, blood pressure, and calories lost while they racked up fictitious kilometres climbing fictitious mountains. Geneviève stood at their sides to motivate them, one two three four, keep up the pace. The young executives on the make looked at her breasts and pedalled faster and faster, while she turned her loveliest smiles on them, as if suggesting that she'd be the ultimate reward for their race. Pedal faster, gentlemen, if you want to demolish your squash racquets and your opponents, if you want to be competitive in business and top performer in love.

Sacrifice, hard work, discipline, productivity, competitiveness, excellence, performance, total quality at all times, even in bed. How long must we keep this up? And what if they were all wrong — her father, her teachers, the businessmen, the journalists and politicians, the commentators and fine talkers, what if everyone was wrong and they should be slowing down instead of speeding up?

Slow down. Geneviève stopped then, abruptly. She'd walked so quickly and for so long that she couldn't recognize the street she was on. Lost in thought, she had strayed from her usual route, which never took her more than five minutes from her apartment, as if she were held by an invisible leash. Reflexively, she took her pulse. A hundred and twenty beats a minute. For Christ's sake, why?

Then she went home, slowly. *There's no rush, it would be ridiculous to get arrested for speeding.* She threw her apartment door wide open and, instead of touring her hiding places, went to the plaster figurines bravely standing guard on their bookshelf. She touched the ox's muzzle with her finger, as if to feel its warm breath, then went to the bathroom and filled the tub with hot water and scented foam.

No, she wouldn't turn the money over to the police. That would be really dumb. No one was ever going to track her down. But she couldn't spend the rest of her days pacing her apartment. Or go back to Le Pussy, to say nothing of the fitness centre. What, then?

Breathe deeply, blow on the foam to make holes in it; uncover a knee or a toe, then let it get covered with bubbles again. Close your eyes, slip into the water up to your neck, don't try to reason with the first, the second, the small *a*, the small *b*, let it come, let it happen, let yourself dissolve in the water, heaven is a bubble bath, things happen, that's all, and afterwards you try to compromise; things happen, yes, and then they sometimes work out strangely; a memory, an impression, a fragment of conversation, all you have to do is not think about it.

Once upon a time there was a client who climbed fictitious mountains at the fitness centre, who gave her his business card. Fifty dollars an hour, total security, if you're ever interested, it's a show, just a show, they look but they don't touch, there's less risk of an attack if you work for us than if you walk down the street. She'd kept the card in her wallet, just in case, and she'd found it when she dismissed the young man she'd been living with; she still had to pay the rent, that or something else....

Six months at Le Pussy. Exhausting work, disgusting sometimes, but it paid. She could have got used to it, gone on for another few years and accumulated enough to pay for a condo in Greece. A small car, the sun, the beach; all the girls at Le Pussy dreamed about such things. But the reality was that she'd have ended up like those little old ladies who stuff themselves with sleeping pills to forget about the money they've hidden under their mattresses. Money, trophies: is there nothing else?

She'd wanted to blow something up. Place dynamite in a night deposit vault, for instance. Little Robert had taught her how, the cops who were regulars at Le Pussy had admitted that it was an excellent idea.... One big bang and that would be the end of Le Pussy. She had used her days off to locate the night deposit vault, buy the dynamite, learn how to handle it. She had mentally repeated every movement during her shows, asking herself each time if she could really do it, telling herself it was better than listening to that goddamn taped music, the panting clients, and the tearing of paper towels.

And she'd done it. She'd progressed from seven dollars an hour to fifty, then from fifty to two hundred and fifty thousand. And after that? How much longer did she have to keep this up?

Getting out of the tub, Geneviève unthinkingly opened the bottle of sleeping pills. She placed a tablet on her tongue, then immediately spat it out. No, not tonight. No more sleeping pills or Valium, no more living like a little old lady. Let's not rush, though; one thing at a time. First of all, find a way to launder the money; then see about organizing the second part of her life.

She didn't yet know exactly how she'd get there, but she knew that she would; that night, for the first time in a long while, Geneviève slept like a log, and didn't dream about either the gutted safe or the clients at Le Pussy.

CHAPTER 5

Brodeur had spent hours studying lengthy computer lists, without much success, and now he had his eye on the percolator wheezing on the kitchen counter. This percolator that she'd given him for his birthday, a few lightbulbs, and the box of baking soda at the back of the fridge were the only things Suzanne had left. The TV set, stereo system, CD collection, the sheets and towels and everything else, she'd taken without the slightest scruple.

When he called her, after the storm had blown over, to ask if she intended to pay her share of the hydro bill for the previous two months, Suzanne sent him packing: "I see you're as mean as ever."

And so he'd paid them all, including the two-thousand-dollar municipal tax bill — after all, he wasn't going to bother Suzanne over something so minor — and then he'd gone into debt up to his neck to buy new furniture. He could have replaced the percolator at the same time — what was another two hundred dollars at that point? — but he had resisted the temptation. Why throw out a nearly new appliance just to buy another one exactly like it? And wasn't there something therapeutic about gazing day after day at this beautiful nickel-plated object, this little bomb that spat out bursts of steam?

Brodeur downed his fifth coffee of the day — it was

barely eleven a.m. — and glanced at the kitchen table: an overflowing ashtray, some sheets of paper covered with notes, a file containing the experts' report, and the endless computer list he'd strained his eyes over for two long weeks, even on his days off, to no avail. A neat little investigation, though, to which he'd devoted twelve packages of cigarettes, six litres of undrinkable office coffee, and two of espresso, all with no result except that he was able, now and then, to forget Suzanne.

The general call he'd sent out to his colleagues on the night of the robbery had brought him nothing he didn't know already. The three men who had attacked the night deposit vault of a bank in Joliette a month earlier, by bulldozing the wall, had been chased by two patrol cars and caught in a police roadblock. On the night of December 19, all three were locked up in the Baie-Comeau jail. He had also been alerted to an epidemic of thefts of safes, all of them committed in South Shore supermarkets, using Wild West methods; in less than a minute the thieves managed to shatter a window, smash the cash registers with a crowbar, overturn some displays along the way, and make their getaway with the safe. Twelve such robberies later, the crooks were still at large.

Brodeur had kept in touch with his colleagues who were working on that case, but he hadn't stayed on the trail. His own robbers were more discreet, even taking the trouble of sweeping away their footprints. According to the experts' report, they had used an Oscar brand pink plastic broom manufactured in the hundreds of thousands. Unless you were an immigrant newly arrived from Africa, you wouldn't get on the road at this time of year without something like this. One could assume, therefore, that the use of it had not been premeditated. Just a flash as they were leaving the scene. A flash that would have vanished immediately in a brain running on alcohol and coke. But his thieves had gone to the trouble of sweeping the snow. They were sober, calm, methodical. Nothing like the usual bunch of savages.

Brodeur spent long hours peering at his computer screen, making full use of G-12's database. He had only to tap some keys to learn that those born under the sign of Scorpio were overrepresented in the category of rapists, or that the average height of pederasts was slightly above normal. If you were looking for something useful, though, you'd never find it; he had carefully sifted through every bank and safe heist committed in Quebec, New Brunswick, and eastern Ontario during the past year, concentrating his search on the key words "dynamite and various explosives," but he hadn't found a word about sandbags. Of the hundreds of suspects questioned, no explosives specialist, not even someone who'd worked as a sweeper at a CIL plant, had been found.

No theft of dynamite had been reported in the previous three months but, all the same, he had taken the trouble of visiting every permit-holder in the region. It's fairly easy for a construction worker to swipe a couple of sticks with no one the wiser. A theft that goes unnoticed, a boss who's careless about his inventory or forgets to notify the police.... So he surveyed every construction site in the surrounding area, with no results. That probably meant that the thieves had got their dynamite on the black market. Waiters in certain bars take strange orders: "Two beers, one girl, one gram of coke, two sticks of dynamite, and a machine gun? Right away, sir. For here or to take out?"

By good fortune only one newspaper, which specialized in such stories, had reported the robbery, and the article had been a model of sobriety. According to the reporter, the thieves had got away with just two or three thousand half-charred dollars, as the vault had been emptied moments before the robbery was committed. There was obviously no mention of the sandbags: freedom of information is one thing, incitement to crime another. This treatment had cut down considerably on the number of anonymous calls, all of which had come from the immediate area. Only one had seemed promising. An employee of the Caisse Populaire in the next village had advised police that one of his customers, who usually cashed only his social assistance cheques, had for several weeks been stepping up his cash deposits. Brodeur went straight to the suspect's house and discovered a large amount of contraband liquor in his garage. That day, at least, hadn't been totally wasted.

The round of hotels and businesses in the village having been equally futile, he'd spent the rest of the time going over and over his computer lists, looking for an engineering graduate, a former FLQ terrorist, someone who sold sandboxes — anything at all. The method isn't as silly as it sounds; searching for anything at all, or even *not* searching, is sometimes what sets off a little spark in a foggy brain.

And so, two weeks after the robbery, an idea had forced its way into Brodeur's mind — one that contradicted everything his experience had taught him, but couldn't be eliminated without further examination: the robbery might well have been the work of a lone thief. A man on his own, with nerves of steel. He parks his car in front of the vault, leaves the motor running, quietly deposits the bags of sand, then the two sticks of dynamite; he plugs his ears, then gathers up the bags, sweeps away his footprints, and so long, byebye. Such tactics would let him go on indefinitely, confident that he'd never be turned in by an accomplice. Why deprive himself of the chance to do the same thing again? He'd develop a taste for it, inevitably, and he wouldn't necessarily always be so lucky. All Brodeur had to do was wait for a repeat performance.

And one day or another he'd spill the beans. A man can be quiet for a few weeks, a few months at most, especially if he works alone, but in the end he always wants to talk to his drinking buddies, or his girlfriend, or a bartender, a barber — even a priest, if there's still one to be found. A man who has succeeded at something has to flaunt his trophy, or he's not a real man. What's the good of winning if nobody knows?

Even if he accomplished the feat of not saying anything, one day or another he'd have to spend his stash. Two hundred and fifty thousand dollars, even in small bills, leaves traces in a bank account, and even more in the hearts of family, friends, and acquaintances. "How did he manage to buy himself a Camaro? He didn't win the lottery, we'd have heard. There's something funny about it, don't you think?" No one is absolutely alone, and all it takes is an unexpected sum of money coming in for prying parents, supposed best friends, an ex-wife wanting to adjust her alimony, and dozens of hitherto unknown brothers-in-law to come out of the woodwork. And that's when the phones start ringing. Clues, fingerprints, and brilliant deductions belong in detective novels. In real life, the police are happy with anonymous calls from envious brothers-in-law.

In the meantime, you can always drop the computer list to the floor like a Slinky. Or crumple up pages covered with hypotheses and pitch them into the wastebasket, awarding yourself two points per successful pitch. Resist the urge to make more coffee, and go to the bathroom and take a Zantac instead. Think about what the doctor said: You're young, M. Brodeur, to start collecting ulcers. You should stop smoking. And avoid irritants: coffee, tomato juice, alcohol, pickles. *And Suzanne*, Brodeur had thought.

Suzanne, whose career had taken off like a rocket and who'd jettisoned him as if he had never been anything but an external fuel tank, now useless and cumbersome, on the very day he'd asked her to marry him. Suzanne, who was now sharing a lawyer's bed. Hang in there, Suzanne, you'll land yourself a judge, maybe even a cabinet minister.

Lie down on the living-room sofa and try to nap. No music, no TV, only silence. Suzanne hated silence. She had to have her Led Zeppelin tapes, always, and coffee, and cigarettes, and work she brought home, and advanced courses — so many that she then had to sign up for stress-management workshops that she had a hard time fitting into her agenda. Brodeur practically had to make an appointment to talk about marriage. "Marriage? Are you kidding? You really want me to put on weight?" Talk about an answer. Know what, Suzanne? A little weight wouldn't have hurt you.

One thing at a time: first, cut out coffee. Then cigarettes. Stay on the sofa, close your eyes, and do nothing. How about getting a cat? Good idea, yes; Suzanne was allergic. And wait. Because someone, somewhere, is going to talk.

CHAPTER 6

"You know, I sometimes get a weird premonition about Geneviève."

Monique Vallières had absent-mindedly glanced at the clock radio, which showed twenty past midnight; then she'd turned towards her husband, who had barely got his breath back after spending some time clearing his throat. It's a strange thing, the human machine; never, ever did her husband cough during their embrace. Afterwards, systematically, he would be overcome by a long coughing fit, as if he were freeing his cough after hoarding it for too long; and then, without a word, he'd fall asleep. Monique wasn't offended. After thirty years of marriage, one can dispense with the obligatory State of the Relationship exchange. And why wait for the protection of night to talk about the children when they've left home long ago? Monique had quickly come around to her husband's arguments, especially after she stopped smoking. She too liked to fall asleep gently. In fact, she was just about to spin herself some dainty dreams when Bernard, instead of turning onto his side and curling up for sleep, remained on his back, looking up at the ceiling, and talked about his weird premonition. Monique had guessed that he had something on his mind, but the last thing she suspected was that he was thinking about his daughter.

"You aren't saying anything...."

"Sorry, Bernard, I was falling asleep.... You said something about Geneviève? What is it you're worried about?"

"If you want to sleep it can wait till tomorrow."

"No, it's all right, I'm awake now."

Thus Bernard confirmed once again the two chief advantages of marriage to a psychologist: because of her job Monique felt obliged to like sex, which meant that he could put up with a lot of minor annoyances; and, equally impressive, he never caught her not listening.

"I phoned her place a while ago. She wasn't there."

"So? At her age she's entitled to go out on Saturday night...."

"That's just it, that's what I'm worried about. Is it really over with her and Guillaume?"

"Yes, absolutely. It's been six months since he packed up and left. From what she told me, there's nobody else in her life. No one serious, anyway. Don't tell me you miss him!"

"Why not? I think he's worth getting to know."

"Of course he's worth getting to know, he's a carbon copy of you. Uncommunicative, stubborn, grouchy, emotionally detached. Physically too, it's quite striking: a receding hairline at his age...."

"Let's not get into that again. You know perfectly well we were like cat and dog."

"Because you were so much alike. What I think is that Geneviève finally realized she'd chosen a younger version of her father. Her spirit of rebellion was stronger. The second child...."

Sitting cross-legged on the bed, Monique was alluding once again to the latest fashionable theory, which maintained that personality is determined by birth order: the eldest child inherits the role of hero, the second is doomed to perpetual rebellion, the third retreats into silence, the fourth plays the clown — and then it starts all over again.

Bernard was listening abstractedly and musing that his

son, Louis, corresponded perfectly to the model: captain of his hockey team, winner of numerous tennis tournaments, brilliant commerce student — a genuine champion. Right after graduation he'd got a job with Bombardier, where he was quickly ascending the ranks. At twenty-five, he already owned a house in Boucherville with a heated pool and a huge flagstone carport big enough for two cars, the second one belonging to Véronique, the sort of wife who climbs up on the platform behind you, whom you place at your side but slightly behind, so she can smile graciously while you deliver your speech. Once the ceremony is over, you can deflate her and stow her in your briefcase. The kind of wife Monique could have become if she hadn't got it into her head at thirty-five to study psychology.

Louis was a high achiever, and competitive. A hero, yes, and why not? There are plenty of losers in this country, we needn't feel obliged to turn out more. But why did Monique insist on placing Geneviève among the rebels? Granted, she hadn't done as well at school as Louis. It even seemed that she'd taken a perverse pleasure in embarking on dead-end paths. After sampling literature and Spanish — a mere three courses, that was all — she'd finally decided to try for the most pathetic diploma, a certificate actually, not even a BA, in phys ed. He had restrained himself from expressing even a hint of approval, for fear that she'd react by giving up again.

A kind of revolt, or rather, passive resistance; yes, it could be. All things considered, Bernard would have preferred the classic reaction: sex and drugs and rock 'n' roll. Like so many others, he'd been there and it hadn't killed him. It's straightforward, it's clear, and it leaves pleasant memories.

Geneviève a rebel? But against whom, exactly? While she was often at odds with her mother (maybe they were too much alike, thought Bernard with a vindictive snicker), her relationship with him had been fairly harmonious overall, with some lovely moments of affection. Rebellious, his little Geneviève, so slight that you had to hold her firmly by the hand on days when the wind was strong lest she blow away? The girl who, in the midst of her adolescent crisis, sometimes came and laid her head on his shoulder? Get serious.

Monique was still talking, stringing together anecdotes aimed at proving that, from the minute she was born, Geneviève couldn't tolerate authority. In fact, she was quite sure that was why their daughter hadn't wanted to spend Christmas with them. Twenty-two years old and she still thinks she has to rebel against every tradition....

"If she wants to spend Christmas by herself, it's her business. She said she had a migraine, didn't she?"

"A migraine! Did you believe that? Poor Bernard, you're awfully naive."

"Maybe I am, but I know how to count."

"What do you mean?"

"Exactly what I said. It's not her psychology I'm worried about, or what she did on Christmas night, it's her finances."

"Her finances?"

"Yes, her finances. When she was living with Guillaume it was all right, though I often wondered how they could keep up their lifestyle. Now she's been on her own for six months but she still manages to pay her rent — that's at least seven hundred a month — and her car..."

"A Honda Civic isn't a Rolls-Royce..."

"It's still a new car. Three hundred a month plus insurance. Which adds up to a thousand a month. Plus clothes, food, car expenses, hydro, everything else. How can she make ends meet with a little job at a Nautilus centre? Are you giving her money?"

"No."

"Neither am I. Have you any idea how much an instructor in a gym earns? Seven or eight dollars an hour, max. No matter how you add it up, it's not enough."

"So what do you think she's doing? Selling crack in

schoolyards?"

"No, that's not her style."

"What then?"

"Look.... Do you have any proof she's working at Nautilus?"

"Proof? Why should I have proof? That's what she told us, isn't it?"

"True. She *told* us she was working at a Nautilus centre, but she never talks about it. Do you think that's normal, somebody who never talks about their work?"

"She never talks about much in any case. But what are you getting at?"

"Just this: I tried to call her this morning. I wanted to invite her for lunch on your birthday. She wasn't home. Then I tried calling her at work. Since I didn't have her number, I called every single Nautilus centre in the area, even the head office. Nobody'd ever heard of Geneviève Vallières. She's never worked in a Nautilus centre."

"Why would she make that up?"

"Because she's hiding something. How do you think a young woman of twenty-two, a pretty woman too, I have to say, can afford that rent and a new car and everything else? A young woman who doesn't work but who's never home in the evening?"

"You mean you think she...."

"I didn't say that. There are thousands of...of dancers in Quebec. Downtown, you can't take two steps without.... Little girls of twenty, from normal families like ours. On the one hand, unemployment and social assistance or little dead-end jobs; on the other hand, easy money, the good life.... I'm not positive, mind you, it's just a hunch, but it's been on my mind."

"Geneviève?"

Torrents of images flooded Monique's brain, each more horrible than the one before: a smoke-filled room reeking of stale beer; dumb brutes, panting and drooling with desire, are watching Geneviève sway, naked, on a small stage;

one of the brutes, in a torn undershirt, stinking of sweat, beer in hand, drops his pants while Geneviève gets down on her knees....

Seized by vertigo, Monique reached out reflexively to her bedside table for a pack of cigarettes. She groped for a while before resigning herself to switching on the lamp, as if to justify her movement. One act led to another, and she got up and pulled on her bathrobe.

"What are you doing?"

"I have to go to the bathroom. I'll be right back."

Monique would never have dared to admit that she simply wanted to be alone for a few moments. While there are undeniable advantages to being married to a Jesuit-educated lawyer, not the least of which is living in a magnificent house in Saint-Bruno, there are a number of drawbacks too: even after thirty years of marriage, Monique could never think properly in the presence of her husband. Instead of going to the upstairs bathroom, where she usually went to get a grip on herself when they had minor disagreements to settle, she went to the one on the main floor, at the other end of the house.

After first splashing her face with water and then choking down a few mouthfuls, she sat on the toilet seat. Covering her face with her hands to help her concentrate, she did her best to evoke the appalling images, one by one: Geneviève wriggling in front of some old perverts, Geneviève kneeling before a brute....

She'd taken the same steps a few years earlier, when her husband admitted to a long affair with another lawyer in his department. In the end she'd admitted that the images were believable, even though she hadn't suspected a thing. But for her daughter to.... Once again she overcame her disgust and tried to imagine her little Geneviève in some dingy hotel, offering her body for a few dollars.... No, it was impossible, absolutely impossible. A wife may be blind, but a mother, a real mother, would have sensed such a thing.

Her husband had managed once again to drag her into

one of those disputes that were a specialty of his. Bernard had always had an unfortunate obsession with entangling her in his twisted arguments, and he was never satisfied till he could snare her in his web. You have to watch out for these lawyers who climb the rungs of the legal departments in big corporations without ever having to plead, and who make up for it by acting out great trials in their private lives.

Monique got up to drink some more cold water and then, as she stood at the mirror and stared herself straight in the eyes, repeated that she was a university graduate too, so she was not without resources, and that, frankly, it was high time she got over her complexes. Thus equipped, she was ready to pursue the conversation on equal terms.

She went back up to the bedroom, hoping with all her heart that Bernard hadn't fallen asleep while she was gone — something he was quite capable of doing. To her surprise, the bed was empty.

She didn't find her husband upstairs or downstairs. Increasingly worried (she actually had time to imagine the car running in the tightly sealed garage), she finally found him in the basement, in the billiard room. Slumped in a leather armchair and holding a Scotch, he was gazing at the shelves where Louis's trophies and Geneviève's photos were lined up.

"What are you doing down here?"

His only reply was to twirl the glass slowly and, looking lost, study the waltz of the ice-cubes.

"Now look," said Monique, instinctively employing the drawling voice she used with agitated patients, "I've been mulling over what you told me and I think you were wrong to imagine anything like that. There's one crucial point all the studies agree on: ninety percent of the girls who do that kind of work have been victims of incest or sexual assault, they've got zero self-esteem and they think they're worth next to nothing; that isn't Geneviève. And there's something in your argument that doesn't add up. If I remember correctly, Geneviève has always said that she works in *a kind of* Nautilus centre. There are lots of other fitness centres, aren't there? Poor Bernard, you've built a whole theory out of nothing. And I've got my own idea about all this."

"You know where she's working?"

"No, but I know what's working on you. Psychologists have known for a long time that children are repelled by the thought of their parents having sex. Even though they're the living proof of it, they reject the evidence, or rather they refuse to see it. What's not so well known, and specialists have been looking into it for a while now, is that the reverse is also true. Parents have a lot of trouble admitting that their children have sex lives. When Louis..."

"I never had trouble imagining Louis's sex life!"

"Because he's your son. There's a certain complicity between males. You might even feel a sort of vicarious pride. But it's different for a father and his daughter. I used to react the same way when Louis brought girls home. I did my best to try to imagine what they were up to in the basement, but I couldn't. There was a kind of block in my mental images, I don't know if you see what I'm trying to say...."

Bernard was listening distractedly to what Monique had to say while he finished his Scotch. He had to admit, her argument about the Nautilus centre that wasn't had some merit, but Bernard was still only half-reassured. Nautilus or not, it was hard to explain Geneviève's lifestyle. And if it's true that ninety percent of the girls who do that kind of work have been assaulted during childhood, that still leaves ten percent who are normal, who just want to pay for their education or buy themselves a little luxury or leave the countryside and move to the city, and Monique was in a good position to know; they used to be called topless waitresses and you could find them all over, even in Chicoutimi. Say whatever you want, Monique, and dress it up in your finest jargon, it still sounds fishy.

CHAPTER 7

"If you ask me, it's just a snag in his love life. It happens."
"A snag that's lasted six months? I mean, okay, so Geneviève's a dish, but there're plenty of Genevièves around.
You just have to go out and keep your eyes open. Couldn't it be a dope problem?"

Alex and Francis, who had started the conversation, were moving around the pool table, which was lit by two hanging lamps whose beams swallowed their cigarette smoke as if they were chimneys. Raphaël was sitting in an easy chair facing the modular shelf unit that filled one whole wall of the basement and housed the giant-screen TV, tape deck, and stereo system. Bending over the small packet he'd just opened, he didn't say a word — the slightest breath might send the precious powder flying — but he didn't miss a word the other two were saying.

"No, I'm telling you, it's his love life. The guy's used to getting what he wants. But Geneviève kicked him out and now he has to come to grips with it."

"I always thought she was a little slow, his Geneviève. Okay, so his heart's been battered a little, I feel his pain, but to wander around like a lost soul.... Have you seen him lately? A ghost, man! Maybe the dope screwed up something in his brain — like, disconnected some neurons, burned out the circuits...."

"Why not a blown fuse, while you're at it? That's not it. Besides, he doesn't do anything any more, not even hash." "You're both wrong. It isn't dope and it isn't his love life either. It's religion."

Alex and Francis immediately stopped playing and turned towards Raphaël, who had just divided the little mound of white powder into four absolutely equal lines on the coffee table. As a reward for his labour, he was sniffing the edges of his American Express card.

Immediately the others replaced their cues in the rack and drew up in silence, moving like cosmonauts, afraid that the slightest draft would destroy their friend's patient work. They examined the perfectly identical furrows in the garden of snow that was reflected in the black glass of the table and then, after a questioning look at one another, agreed that once again Raphaël had done a remarkable job. Nothing surprising about it; the one who divided up the powder snorted the last line — an incentive to observe the strictest equity. Kneeling around the table, Alex and Francis took their share and waited impatiently for Raphaël to do the same.

"Religion?" Alex and Francis then repeated in unison.

Alex, who had just stuffed his nose, kept his eyes shut, forehead resting on his joined hands. He was thinking about the stupid trick that had been played on him at Scout camp: someone had come into the dorm one night and tied together, into a huge knot it took the campers a whole day to untangle, all the laces in all their shoes and boots. He often felt that cocaine knotted his synapses together in the same way. Religion.... Alex and Francis were waiting for a response.... Raphaël was delighted at having held their attention for so long, but he hadn't the faintest idea how to keep it. In fact, why did he have this hunch?

"Explain what you mean. We're waiting."

"I was thinking about my mother when she had her drinking problem. She tried everything. Acupuncture, therapy, psychoanalysis, crystals, tisanes.... She finally ended up in church. Since then she's been going to mass every Sunday. She even burns candles at home. Just imagine if people found out. The great lawyer, the divorce specialist, burning votive candles...."

"Did it work?"

"Nope. Still drinks like a fish."

"And what's that got to do with Guillaume?"

"Who knows?"

All three giggled, and no doubt would have shrugged and gone back to their game if Alex, his eyes glued to the table, hadn't stopped them.

"Hang on, something's weird."

Raphaël felt a spurt of adrenalin rising; was Alex on to him? Whenever he divided up the powder, he first rubbed his credit card against his pants to charge it with static electricity, which meant that he got an extra hit when he sniffed the edges.

"Look at the table...."

Raphaël followed the gaze of the other two and peered at the useless little line still waiting to be snorted. Why had he divided it in four when there were only three of them? He stammered something to justify himself (it's your fault too, you're always talking about Guillaume), then looked towards the chair where Guillaume's ghost still sat — that damn ghost who persisted in haunting them.

§

Guillaume wouldn't have accepted the religious hypothesis either. The meaning of existence was the least of his concerns. He didn't believe that something in his brain was broken, nothing irreparable anyway. He was in love, that was all. It happens.

And it can take many forms. For instance, you can be in love without knowing it, which was precisely what had happened to Guillaume at the age of sixteen, when he first met Geneviève, in the tritest way you could imagine. She was a neighbour. The neighbour you take to the movies, shyly, and then she invites you back to her place one evening when her parents are out. The one you share the first joint with, the first fumblings. The one who, after many futile attempts, receives your first premature ejaculations. And the one you accompany to the drugstore, worried sick, to get the results of the pregnancy test.

Guillaume and Geneviève had split up after a year, by common consent, both convinced — because they'd seen too many movies and read too many novels — that no genuine love story could start in such a banal way. They'd decided to look elsewhere, in case love could be measured, and then to compare notes.

You can also be in love by default. Every time he was disappointed by what he'd seen elsewhere, every time he was tired of biting and clawing and wanted attention and rest, he phoned Geneviève. Often all she did was listen to him, if she herself was busy elsewhere. But sometimes, when by chance their breakups coincided, they'd gone on together for a little while — a few days, a few weeks, sometimes a few months.

Which was how they'd come to rent the apartment where they'd lived for six months, without ever talking about love or plans for the future — but also without even a hint of bickering or shouting.

Guillaume was at university, Geneviève was teaching young executives on the make how to harden their abdominal muscles, and they got together in the evening like a perfectly ordinary couple. They'd do the dishes listening to music, then watch television or plunge into a good thick novel, side by side. Those are the things they never show in movies, which may explain why people don't know how to take advantage of them. Later on, when you've fallen in love after the fact, those little nothings are what you miss.

Many times Guillaume had rerun the film of those few months in the hope of finding the minor event, the awkward little remark that had made everything collapse.

That evening they talked about their future. More precisely, Guillaume talked about it. For some obscure reason, the word seemed to have been banished from Geneviève's vocabulary. He said that he intended to go to the States for an MA, to Chicago maybe, or Harvard. After that he might go to England. Geneviève could follow him. What difference would it make if she was working in Montreal, the States, or England? She'd see some of the country and she could take courses. How could a girl of her calibre be satisfied with a diploma in phys ed?

She said nothing, but he sensed that something had been broken, that she'd gone into her shell. And then everything came undone, until the day she told him to pack his bags. No big scene, no anger, no argument even; that was the way it was, it was nobody's fault, there was nothing to understand.

And ever since that day, Guillaume had been in love after the fact. His condition seemed irreversible. The mere thought of looking elsewhere, even to give himself a different outlook, seemed to him pure heresy. He couldn't stroll down the street any more, or go to a movie or even walk into a store, without imagining that he would run in to her, that they'd go for a coffee, that they'd finally be able to explain themselves, and everything would be as it had been before.

Guillaume was in love after the fact, it happens, and it means that you have no desire to get together with old friends around a pool table, playing at who's the biggest cynic.

Anyone who has been afflicted with that malady knows that it makes you act strange. You wander aimlessly through the city streets, picking the busiest one in the hope of provoking fate. And if fate refuses to make an effort, you try to force its hand by spending your time in all the places where the loved one hangs out; then you inevitably go out of your way just to walk past her house. And if you do run in to her, you just have to feign surprise, stammer whatever occurs to you, and invite her for a coffee.

As it will be very hard to appear natural in these circumstances, and as you'll feel a little ashamed, you'll walk very fast, with your head down. You'll barely raise your eyes as you go by her door, to see if there's a light in the living-room or bedroom.

A few blocks away, you call from a pay phone and hang up as soon as you hear her voice. You walk some more, for a long time, wondering if it wouldn't have been better, in the end, to hear a rival's voice. If a girl leaves you to go and live with another girl, you can accept it, eventually; after all, you can't transform yourself into something you aren't. If she prefers another man to you, you can take that too; at least it gives you someone to hate, so you haven't lost everything. But if she leaves you to live by herself, if she prefers nothing at all to you, that makes you less than nothing.

What can she be doing all by herself in that big empty apartment?

And then you go home, you pace, you want to get things clear in your own mind, you go to the telephone and punch in — very quickly, for fear that you'll change your mind — the number of the last person you'd have thought of contacting in such circumstances.

CHAPTER 8

After he finished law school, Bernard Vallières had been taken on by one of the biggest firms in the land and had immediately embarked on a long climb that had brought him to the top of the hierarchy. Which meant that he knew the drill. Even at the peak of his career, though, he could never get used to the ritual of the business lunch. To his methodical mind there was something barbaric about putting those two words together; the finest dishes taste insipid when you share them with a boring client, bread-crumbs inevitably get stuck between the calculator keys, and when you reread it at leisure the contract turns out to be spangled with trick clauses and wine-stains.

When Guillaume contacted him, though, he didn't hesi-tate to invite him to lunch; the matter they would be deal-ing with was strictly private and a restaurant would be more suitable — all right, then, let's say a quarter to twelve?

After he hung up, Bernard paced his office, unable to concentrate on work. What could Guillaume possibly want from him? Surely he hadn't phoned his ex-girlfriend's father to ask for a summer job or to discuss his career plans. His strictly private matter obviously had something to do with Geneviève; what else did they have in common, if one could put it that way?

Was Guillaume going to confide in him, was he expecting advice to help him get back together with her? That was idiotic; in a pinch you can talk about such things with a girl's mother, but not with her father. If Guillaume wanted to pour his heart out he should speak to Monique. Psychologists, as everybody knows, always pad their shoulders with little sponges. That left just one hypothesis: that Guillaume had his own suspicions and wanted to sort them out. And so he'd taken the bull by the horns and called Bernard. All in all, Monique might not have been wrong when she said Guillaume resembled him.

At eleven-thirty, unable to wait any longer, Bernard was already seated in the restaurant, fidgeting in his chair, tearing open the envelopes of soda crackers and nibbling at them, pulling fragments of crust off the bread, and turning to the door whenever a new customer came in.

When Guillaume finally showed up, at twelve minutes to noon, Bernard shook hands with him, horribly uncomfortable; this twenty-two-year-old, who looked sixteen with his curly hair and his big round eyes, might be innocence personified, but he was still his daughter's former lover.

Guillaume was just as embarrassed; he'd always seen Geneviève's father as a strange and dangerous competitor who had to be treated like a wounded old lion curled up in his den.

Bernard had ordered two Scotches, as much to break the ice as to establish his authority; there's nothing like giving a waiter orders to restore your self-confidence. Guillaume barely had time to sit down before the drinks were on the table.

"I'm sure you're wondering..."

Bernard stopped him with a wave of his hand, then brought his drink to his lips, forcing Guillaume to do the same. Easy does it, young fellow. Let me lead the way. First some small talk, to give us time to study the angle of attack, then we look at the menu, and while we're doing that we draw up our strategy....

"I wanted to talk to you about Geneviève. No matter

how hard I try, I can't figure out what happened."

Since he can't stop talking, thought Bernard, might as well try to control him. For a start, put things in context.

"You haven't been living together for a while now, is that right?"

"Yes. It's been six months..."

"And you haven't seen her at all?"

"No — I mean yes, once, when I went to pick up my things. I tried to talk to her, I wanted her to explain..."

"You wanted to understand why she dropped you?"

"Of course. But there's more. Actually, if you want to know what's really on my mind, I've been wondering how she's getting by. Financially, I mean."

Though Bernard had seen it coming, he had trouble swallowing his Scotch.

"What do you mean, exactly?"

His voice was uncertain, his tone falsely innocent; the old lion had lost something of his haughtiness, and now Guillaume, who didn't miss a thing, brought his glass to his lips, forcing Bernard to do the same. I know the drill too. If you think I'm going to let you manipulate me.... He took another sip of Scotch — to savour his victory, but also to embolden himself. It was time to plunge in, and he had trouble stepping up to it.

"Look, Guillaume, I can't waste my time. If you've got something to say, say it."

"I'm getting there. The problem is simple. When we were living together we didn't have any financial worries. My parents always helped me, Geneviève was working, and I had summer jobs..."

"Sorry to interrupt, but where was she working, exactly?"

"At a fitness centre, like a Nautilus centre."

"Not a real Nautilus centre?"

"No, it was a small independent set-up, in Longueuil. Didn't you know that?"

"She told me about it, of course, but.... You say she *was*

working — you mean she isn't now?"

"No, at least not at the same place. When I phoned they told me she'd resigned. They didn't know anything more."

The old lion's questions were annoying Guillaume a lot more than he'd expected. At this point he didn't mind if he lost the thread. On the contrary, he hoped he'd lose it, as Bernard most likely did; he'd long since finished his drink but still kept bringing his glass to his lips. Was he too feeling the ground open beneath his feet?

"Look, Monsieur Vallières.... I've seen Geneviève's cheque stubs. Three hundred dollars a week. With eight hundred for rent plus everything else, there's a shortfall.... Of course, if you're helping her out..."

"No. She's never accepted a cent. What would you say to a steak?"

"Sure, whatever," replied Guillaume, taken by surprise.

He didn't mind the rather cavalier way in which Bernard was doing his best to take back control. There was even something admirable about the way he'd handled it: a simple movement of the finger, very discreet, and the waiter came running, with much bowing and scraping. "Two steaks. Rare, Guillaume? Two steaks then, rare, and some wine. The best. I trust you." The way he dropped his remarks, patronizingly, his eyes half closed; his certainty that he was doing the waiter a great honour by giving him his trust; and the waiter, ramrod-stiff and oozing servility, rushing to the kitchen as if he'd been entrusted with the most important mission.... Maybe Guillaume would become a man like that too, when he'd lost his hair and he wore thousand-dollar suits.

But, contrary to popular belief, a suit-jacket doesn't hide everything; after he'd given the waiter his order, Bernard's shoulders were hardly any straighter. The therapy hadn't helped much. Though he was already sure that they'd soon reach the same conclusion, Guillaume was hoping with all his heart that it would be the older man who showed his hand.

"She could have won the lottery, of course. But if that's so, why would she hide it? It's no disgrace..."

"I've already thought of that. There aren't all that many solutions: either she's pushing drugs..."

"I can set your mind at rest on that score, Monsieur Vallières. That's not her style. I've never even seen her smoke a joint."

"I know. And it doesn't reassure me in the least, if you really want to know. Because that leaves me with just one hypothesis. What can a twenty-two-year-old woman do to pay a rent of...how much did you say? Eight hundred dollars? That's worse than I thought. I find it hard to believe that Geneviève.... Listen, I'm sure you know that ninety percent of girls who do that kind of work were victims of incest or sexual assault in their childhood. Their self-esteem has taken a beating and..."

"There's still the other ten percent. No, Monsieur Vallières, I might as well lay my cards on the table. Geneviève and I already talked about that. She told me how, one night, one of her clients at the fitness centre made her an offer: fifty dollars an hour to...to dance in front of clients, in a private booth. You can't call that prostitution, I don't think: the girl gets undressed, she puts on a show, but there's no physical contact."

"Yes, I know how it works, I...I've seen reports. And do you really think Geneviève...?"

"I don't have any proof. But I can tell you that I asked her — strictly out of curiosity — if she could ever do that. She thought it over and she said maybe she would, if she really needed the money. I didn't believe her, of course; I mean, it's so degrading. She said it was just a job like any other. I was sure she said that to provoke me."

"Where is it? Where does she do it?"

"I don't know. Look, I don't even know if she's actually done it, it's just a suspicion I've had.... I thought that.... That's what I wanted to tell you, Monsieur Vallières: I've got suspicions, that's all, and I don't know how to shake them off."

"Neither do I, Guillaume, neither do I."

The waiter, sensing that the time had come to break the heavy silence suddenly enveloping their table, brought the wine, which Bernard pretended to taste — you could have poured him the sourest vinegar and he wouldn't have objected — and then the huge steaks that neither of them felt like eating. Still, they cut into them energetically, like children who think that hacking their meat into smaller and smaller pieces will make it disappear.

If they had no appetite for the meat, though, they seemed to be dying of thirst.

They kept talking for a long time, in an undertone, and anyone observing them would surely have wondered about the nature of their relationship; no businessman would talk to a client for so long, a father and son even less.

§

When they'd finished eating, Bernard phoned his secretary, who was very surprised to hear her boss tell her, in a groggy-sounding voice, that his business lunch was taking a lot longer than expected. Then he went to the bathroom, as much to seek some respite as to empty his bladder. He spent longer than usual washing his hands, then looked at himself in the mirror; his face showed the effects of the Scotch and the wine, but he didn't look distraught. After all, Guillaume had told him nothing he didn't already suspect, and anything was better than vague conjecture. He had even discovered in Guillaume an unsuspected ally; to his great surprise, he'd been able to talk to him about his daughter for more than an hour, with absolutely no restraint, and that had done him a great deal of good. He could never have had such a conversation with a man his own age. In his circles, people seemed to consider children either trophies to brag about or shameful diseases. It was better to avoid the subject. And here he'd let himself go on about

Geneviève to a young man who had shared her bed and
wanted nothing more than to do so again, a young man
who'd stolen away his little Geneviève, who was so slight
that you had to hold her hand on days when the wind was
strong.

Guillaume, meanwhile, was calmly sipping his cognac.
If anyone had told him even yesterday that one day he'd
be in this businessmen's restaurant, getting smashed with
his ex-girlfriend's father.... The booze had something to do
with it, no doubt. What else could explain him sharing such
confidences with the man? He could never have acted like
that with his friends Alex, Francis, and Raphaël. If he admitted to them one-tenth of what he'd confided to Bernard,
he'd be the object of their sarcasm to the end of his days.

But if Geneviève found out about it, didn't he risk losing her for ever? The more he thought about it, the more he
told himself he had no choice. No matter what he found
out or how he went about it, he had to know.

CHAPTER 9

Only the CEO of Bernard's firm was entitled to a corner office, which gave him a view of Mount Royal and, on a clear day, the lower Laurentians. Bernard did not envy him these privileges. His own office had just one window, but it looked out on the ever-changing St. Lawrence River with its currents, its ships, and its bridges which sometimes disappeared into the mist. His gaze often wandered beyond the river, skipping from one lonely mountain to another, finally getting lost in the Appalachians on the other side of the border. Even at the height of summer, Vermont always appeared to him as a long gradation from blue to grey, without even a touch of green. Distance might have something to do with it, or pollution, or maybe some tint in the glass, it didn't matter; past Mont Saint-Grégoire the colours faded away. So it was precisely at Mont Saint-Grégoire that the St. Lawrence Valley became adolescent.

This side of Mont Saint-Grégoire, there was a little girl in a world of laughter and bicycles and sundresses and plastic toys floating in a pool.

One day the little girl shut herself inside her bedroom, just for two minutes, long enough to slip into her bathing suit, and Bernard stood by himself outside the locked door, disconcerted and embarrassed to discover that his little girl was now a young woman.

Geneviève had soon got in the habit of shutting herself away for the simple pleasure of being alone and daydreaming, lying on her bed, or talking to her mirror. Who knows what goes on when a teenaged girl shuts her door in your face?

Next, the room was filled with a gang of young girls and all you could hear through the walls was the buzz of their ceaseless chatter, and bursts of laughter for which you'd rather not know the reason.

And then there were no more young girls, only Guillaume, the shy little neighbour boy, and you didn't hear anything at all.

At Mont Saint-Grégoire, all the doors close. The colours fade away and there's nothing in the distance but the hazy mountains. On sunny days you can barely make out their silhouette.

Bernard looked at his enormous desk, on which sat the silent telephone that wouldn't ring again for the rest of the afternoon. "I'm in conference," he'd told the secretary, "screen all my calls — except those from Guillaume. Absolute priority."

Soon, when the effects of the alcohol have worn off, he'll do up his tie and his shoelaces, he'll buckle his belt and go to sit in his swivel chair, facing the empty desk, and his professional reflexes will come back at once. Negotiate, decide, act. That's what he's paid for. And that's why his desk turns its back on the river.

While he waits, he prefers to stay in what designers call the room's social interaction zone, where leather easy chairs are grouped around a low table. Bernard can hold informal discussions with clients and colleagues there, over coffee or Scotch, before moving into the decision-making zone.

When he's alone, he often sits in one of these easy chairs, just to disconnect himself from his work. He takes off his shoes, loosens his tie, gently rubs his temples, and looks at the river, thinking of nothing — or rather, allowing the ideas and images to come, without trying to hold onto them or control them. One fifteen-minute break in the morning, another in the afternoon, and he'll wake up fresh as a daisy, feeling even better than if he'd allowed himself a nap.

It was Monique who, seeing how tense he was one day, suggested taking these relaxation breaks. He shrugged, as usual, but that didn't stop him from implementing her recommendations and enjoying the little daily vacations. Had it occurred to him to thank her? Very likely not. Whenever Monique talked to him he shrugged, as if to plug his ears; but he still repeated her arguments, almost word for word, whenever the opportunity arose.

The second child is doomed to rebel, he'd told Guillaume, who had listened with all the more interest because he was a second child himself and he'd taken great pleasure in telling his parents off at the peak of his adolescence. He'd been an active resister, while Geneviève seemed to have chosen the passive way.... The trail had sounded interesting, but he'd brushed aside the explanation. How could an individual be reduced to a simple matter of birth order? On a scale of the sciences, Guillaume had always put psychology at ground level, only slightly higher than astrology. Since they had plenty of other fish to fry, Bernard had merely smiled at his remark, and they'd gone back to their main topic: the money Geneviève had and the money she didn't have.

It was years ago that she'd stopped accepting money from him, even on her birthday.

In the past there had been birthday cakes, balloons, Christmas trees, gift-wrapped presents, an orgy of colours. Then white envelopes. And then nothing.

The little girl has become a stranger you run into in the morning, with whom you exchange a few banal words: How's school? How are you doing at work? You root around in your memory for something to say, hoping to find an unusual anecdote, some recollection you haven't repeated a thousand times, and you no sooner open your mouth than she shrugs: You sound like a broken record, Papa.

Sometimes, it's true, there are exchanges of nonsense words, of puns, of bright remarks that make her smile and leave you dazzled. And then you don jacket and tie and go to work, happy that you've at least built some bridges between two such distant continents. But while you are signing contracts, mother and daughter are discussing the serious things: the pill, pregnancy tests, a broken heart. The world of laughter and games belongs unofficially to the father; he has to get something, after all.

And then nothing. She tells you that she's leaving to move in with this kid, Guillaume, this clumsy oaf of an adolescent she's never really left, or so it seems. There's no one in the house, which is now too big, and you miss her silences and her closed door.

Whenever she comes home for a meal, you offer her money and she takes offence. How can you make her understand that you're not trying to buy her, that you would simply like to help her out?

You were God Almighty when she was just a child unwrapping her presents under the Christmas tree. You were the devil incarnate when she accepted your money as a teenager. And you're nothing at all when she's become an adult. You go home to your big empty house, and never have you felt so lonely, or so old.

§

Bernard looked at his watch and his tie on the table, his unlaced shoes still sitting on the carpet, and his jacket folded over the back of an easy chair. As soon as he put them on he'd pull himself together, but something held him in this silence where he'd shut himself away in the middle of the afternoon. Through the walls came the muted sounds of ringing telephones, tapping keyboards, the conversations of busy people, and he was still here, slumped in his easy chair, determined to pursue the exploration he'd started by exceeding his fifteen-minute limit. Though motionless, he felt like a child walking alone down the corridors of a school, hearing fragments of French or history or math lessons through the walls. He advanced slowly, frightened by his solitude but at the same time savouring his delinquency.

One day not all that long ago, there had been a woman's shoes on the carpet, silk stockings on the armchair, clothing scattered all over the office, and sweating and sighing and muffled cries. Hélène, VP finance. They would get together at noon, in one office or the other; in the evenings they put in overtime, and they took advantage of every trip and every convention to throw themselves at one another, biting and clawing, furiously. The kind of story that seems so terribly trite when it happens to someone else, and makes you feel so fantastic when it's your turn. The affair had gone on for two years; then Hélène had left to climb other ladders, in another skyscraper. She too was married, with two children close to adolescence.

He confessed everything to Monique and it was months before she came to terms with it. Then they had a long conversation in a restaurant. Monique, who had just gone back to university, had drawn on her psychological jargon so much that Bernard had cramps in his shoulders from shrugging. Translated from the gobbledygook, her remarks did make some sense: Louis was fourteen at the time, and Geneviève twelve. By treating himself to an affair, he'd been trying to conceal his own dismay, to compensate for the power he'd lost in the family, to take revenge on his children by wallowing in his own adolescent crisis.

Bernard, who had only been trying to mend fences, pretended to accept her explanations, but something in him resisted. He had treated himself not so much to an affair, as to a delayed adolescent crisis, though he had felt delinquent in a way. Delinquent, yes — the word sounded strange but it did apply to his situation, as it did to Geneviève's, in fact; she'd always struck him as delinquent in a way, setting herself not *against* the laws but alongside them, elsewhere.

Can't parents treat themselves to a crisis too, a parenting crisis? Refuse to play their role for the duration of an affair, regress the way teens do, test a few more limits before they're too old too soon?

It was long ago, long before anyone had heard about AIDS. Quebec City. A hotel room. Because some day, after all, you had to taste the forbidden fruit; because all his colleagues did, without a hint of shame; because fantasies were tenacious; because he could drop dead the next day; because of all sorts of reasons that were nobody's business but his, once, just once, he'd treated himself to a professional.

Lying on his bed, he had watched a centrefold come to life. He'd never forgotten her perfume, her silk lingerie, her long black hair, her bronze skin, her enticing smile. Miss September; she'd played the game so well you would have sworn she really wanted it. And Bernard had wanted it too, even if he hadn't been able to do a thing.

Though she'd shown an imagination well stocked with treasures and drawn on all her resources, which were many, Bernard couldn't do it. Nothing. Zero. So she got dressed again and Bernard arranged the twenty-dollar bills side by side on the bedside table.

He'd never confessed this episode to Monique, and it had taken him years to admit to himself that never had a sum of money been so well wasted.

Well wasted — yes, particularly since Geneviève was the same age as Miss September.

Geneviève. Miss September. The intolerable connection acted like an electric charge and Bernard sprang from his chair, ready for action. Private eyes didn't exist only in novels; the Yellow Pages listed scads of them. It would cost whatever it cost.

He'd thought of Monique as he was tying his tie. Don't say anything to her. Not just yet.

It wasn't till he was pulling on his jacket that he felt the transformation was finally complete: he was once again a man of decision. Maybe it was a question of fabric, or some mysterious product that tailors sprayed onto businessmen's clothes. At the prices they charged, it was quite possible: you donned a jacket and right away you felt taller, stronger, safe from any kind of attack.

Bernard sat behind his desk and, without giving it too much thought, tried Geneviève's phone number. Why go to a detective when he could conduct his own investigation? A father is entitled to phone his daughter in the afternoon, isn't he?

"Hello?"

The problem, when you're used to answering machines, is that you're always thrown for a loop when you hear a live voice at the other end.

"Geneviève? It's me..."

"Papa? Is something wrong?"

"No, why do you ask?"

"Because it's not like you to phone in the middle of the afternoon. To what do I owe the honour?"

It was a good question, he had to agree. Still slightly dazed, Bernard stammered for a moment before offering her the little lie he'd cooked up:

"It's one of my colleagues.... I ran into him at lunch. He wants to get in shape but there are so many fitness centres he can't sort them out; so I thought I'd refer him to you...."

"Did you talk to Mama about this?"

"No. Why?"

"Because she called last night. It's so weird, she said the very same thing, word for word. A friend who wants to get in shape, she wanted me to give her the address of the gym.... I assume it's a mutual friend."

"I don't think so, it's just a coincidence."

"Pretty funny coincidence. It's as if you're doing an investigation."

"An investigation? Why would I be doing an investigation?"

"I don't know. But you and Mama must be talking to

each other more often; you seem to be on the same wavelength these days."

"Look, Geneviève, I admit it wasn't brilliant, but you're right, it's.... The word 'investigation' is a little strong, but it's something like that. We're both concerned, we want to know if you're still working, if you need money...."

"No, I don't need money. I'm doing just fine where that's concerned.... Too well, even. Papa, can I trust you with a secret?"

"Of course you can."

"I quit my job a while ago. I'd had enough. And at the salary they were paying..."

"I see.... And how are you paying your rent?"

"I've saved some money. I've even got enough to.... Look, can I count on you to keep this secret?"

"Of course you can."

"Okay; I'm thinking of going into business.... Are you still there?"

"Yes, I'm here, but I'm not sure I understood. You, go into business? What kind of business?"

"That's a surprise. Just give me two more weeks and you'll see. Now you'll have to excuse me, I've got an important meeting. Isn't that what people say in your circles, to end a conversation politely? Or should I say a conference?"

"Say conference, that sounds better."

"All right. 'Sorry, but I have to go now, I'm expected at an important conference.' Is that right?"

"Ten out of ten."

"Thank you, sir. Big kiss."

Bernard had often wondered why telecommunications companies, though they were lavish with innovations as varied as they were pointless, had never thought of inventing a tone detector. One glance at a little illuminated screen would let you know if the person you were speaking to was being ironic, sarcastic, weary, faking happiness, bored.... Now he knew the answer: there would be so many screens and such hopping about from one to another that you wouldn't be much farther ahead.

First there'd been suspicion, then a hint of sarcasm, but that wonderful smile in her voice towards the end had made up for everything. Bernard was annoyed with himself for having thought for even a moment about hiring a detective. Maybe he'd have got more precise answers to his questions, but he would have deprived himself of something far more precious: for the first time in years, he had sensed a note of complicity in his daughter's voice. Complicity, that was right, he hadn't been dreaming, and it was worth putting his doubts on ice for that.

Not quite sure what to do with his sudden good mood, he called Monique at her office.

"Bernard? Is anything wrong?"

"Not at all. I know, it's not like me to phone in the middle of the afternoon, but I was wondering if we might eat out tonight. And then go to a movie. How about it?"

This time there wouldn't have been any hopping about from one screen to another, thought Bernard as he listened to Monique's response. Just one would have lit up, to indicate that the woman he was speaking to was absolutely flabbergasted. The long silence that preceded her reply was easy to interpret: help, she must have been thinking, my husband's gone out of his mind.

CHAPTER 10

Geneviève had spent hours going through the classified ads under Businesses for Sale but she hadn't found anything that suited her. Not that her financial expectations were high; it would be enough if the purchase price matched her means and she could sell the business again without too much trouble in a year or two. Whether she might turn a profit or realize a capital gain didn't even cross her mind; it would be enough if most of her customers paid cash and the bookkeeping wasn't too complicated, so that she could deposit a little more money than she'd actually taken in each week.

Every morning she went out to buy the papers and spread them across the kitchen table, where, pen in hand, she conscientiously studied the ads. Proceeding by elimination, she first crossed out businesses that required special skills. Hair and beauty salons, cabinet-making and automotive parts shops were quickly struck off her list. This criterion wasn't absolute, however, since she also crossed out fitness centres, the only field in which she had any expertise.

Some ads set her to dreaming for days. Like the one that offered, in one batch and for a ridiculously low price, a kennel, an obedience school, and a country house. Could

there be any more congenial way to earn your living than
walking quietly along a river lined with willows, throwing
sticks for dogs to retrieve? And who wouldn't feel safe in
that house, where no burglar would dare set foot? Still, she
had to be realistic; a kennel is, first and foremost, a place
where dozens of puppies are cooped up. She'd never be
able to tolerate the smell. So she gave up that idea, regret-
fully, and in light of this new criterion she quickly eliminated pet stores, shoe repair shops, and seniors' homes.

And then another criterion, totally subjective but crucial nonetheless, was added to her list. Any business, no
matter what kind, requires a certain amount of hypocrisy
— something Geneviève, who'd put up with the clients of
Le Pussy for six months, had been paid to know. But she'd
had enough of that. Now what she wanted was a discreet,
polite clientele who wouldn't force her to compromise herself. Anything that remotely resembled a clothing store fell
under the blade, along with bars and restaurants.

In this respect, convenience store customers seemed like
the kind of people she wouldn't mind associating with. Not
all likable, but that would be too much to ask from anonymous individuals who rush in, pay cash, and walk out with
their pack of cigarettes. But the prospect of working a hundred and twenty hours a week didn't thrill her, any more
than handing over the day's receipts to an individual wearing a ski mask and toting a sawed-off shotgun.

Florists, though, are rarely robbed. They work in surroundings that smell good, and there's nothing objection-
able about their hours, and even less about their clientele.
Geneviève tried to picture herself among African violets,
cactuses, crocuses, and coleus; there would also be those
big ungainly plants that drip down all over the place (spi-
der plants?), those red flowers that smell so terrible (gera-
niums?), and all the others.... But no; not having a prodigious memory, she'd never make a credible florist.

And so, for more than two weeks, she searched the
classifieds in all the daily papers without unearthing any-

thing worth a visit or even a phone call. She went on searching, but with no great hope of success, as she'd found it to
be as good a way as any to keep her mind busy. And then,
just as she was beginning to give up hope, she fell on a tiny,
unassuming ad, just four words followed by a phone
number: *Dry-cleaner's for sale*. The sobriety of the text made
her think this could be an excellent sector; no need to attract buyers with promises of an exceptional location, infi-
nite growth potential, or fabulous profits, as was so often
the case with all the restaurants whose owners obviously
wanted to unload them. In fact, there were dozens of restaurants for sale but only one dry-cleaner's.

Geneviève put down her pen and closed her eyes. Customers in a hurry would drop off their pants or skirt in the
morning on the way to their downtown office tower. A little number stapled to an inside seam. A little powder into
the machine, which does the work by itself. Press the pants,
skirts, blouses, wrap them in plastic for the tired customer
who picks them up in the evening just before closing —
and pays cash. Learning the ropes should be easy, the
odours bearable, the clientele decent. You don't sell them
lies or dreams; you provide them with a service, they pay
for it and go on their way, satisfied that their dress no longer
smells of cigarettes or proud of the crisp new crease in their
pants; you accept their money with no remorse — it's clean
money, money you haven't stolen.

And the piles of dirty clothes, and the infernal temperature during heat waves? Cleaners are entitled to take holidays, like everybody else, and business must be slow in
the summer. Who would ever have shorts or bathing suits
dry-cleaned? In the winter, on the other hand....

Then Geneviève remembered the dry-cleaner's shop on
the way to school. She was seven or eight, no more. On
bitingly cold days, she would duck inside that little corner
of desert planted in the snow, like an oasis in reverse, where
she imagined that fragments of cotton or flannel were set-
tling in her lungs to warm them. As long as she behaved

herself, the old man didn't say anything. He even let her dip into the candy dish that sat permanently on the counter.

It takes a very special temperament to spend all day in a steambath, cleaning the grime from other people's clothes, being looked down on by certain customers — but, after all, somebody has to do it. Is there any shame in cleaning clothes? It keeps you busy all day, and you don't risk terminal boredom, like the salesgirls who twiddle their thumbs as they wait for another customer to harass.... But the piles of dirty clothes, the smell of sweat and cigarettes?

Geneviève pursued her reflections while she paced her apartment, sometimes opening her closet to finger her clothes, comparing fabrics and wondering how they had to be cleaned, which at the same time gave her the opportunity to glance at the cardboard boxes packed with money that would also have to be laundered.

She stopped before the plaster ox and ass, as if to ask their advice. Would they feel useless in an overheated crèche? Would they hang in with her for two years? Two years.... She stood frozen there, her finger on the muzzle of the ox: two years. The words resounded like a sentence.

§

Geneviève could have driven for ever along the endless boulevard that stretched from one mall to another, one suburb to another, one city to another, all the way to the limits of America, where automobiles must finally come to an end. For fear of getting lost she had carefully noted her itinerary on a scrap of paper which she consulted at every red light; that kept her from thinking about the situation she was about to get into.

And so she arrived in a neighbourhood that must have been a distant suburb at one time, before it was surrounded by highways and overrun with Burger Kings and Mc-Donalds'. Finally leaving the main artery, she turned onto a long boulevard that eventually took her to a tangle of very short, crescent-shaped streets lined with modest bungalows and ageless duplexes. The sky was grey, the snow was dirty, and the streets were so deserted that the entire landscape looked rather grim. That impression lasted as long as she stayed in her car, but it started to dissipate when she turned off the engine and closed the door. She was early for her appointment, so she decided to get to know what might become her new neighbourhood by strolling slowly, the way you do in the country. The streets were so quiet that she quickly forgot the city and the highways all around. The air was mild that day, but there were only a few passersby, walking their dogs or coming home from shopping with their arms full of groceries. Women of no particular age, not rich or poor or anything else, walking slowly through their delightfully anonymous neighbourhood as if there'd never been anything urgent in their lives.

The church, which must have seemed boldly modern when it was built in the sixties, now resembled a huge, empty shell that might have been abandoned there, as if to serve as a landmark for children, making it easy for them to find their way to school and the playground, and for the old ladies who went to do their shopping at one of those absolutely identical malls that made up a miniature downtown. A video club, a convenience store, a bakery, a menswear store, a family restaurant.... There weren't many customers on this late morning, but none of the premises was empty — a good sign. A fruit store, a unisex hairdresser, an oversize clothing store.... The next store was so repulsive that she nearly passed it by. *One hour Martinizing*. The neon sign, which looked as if it had never worked, was barely readable through a window made opaque by the white mud flung up by automobiles. A yellowing piece of cardboard stuck inside the window advised customers who had not yet taken to their heels that the establishment not only offered that mysterious Martinizing process but also handled leather, suede, and alterations.

The interior was even more repulsive. The walls were covered with fake walnut panelling on which the streaks of grime didn't always blend into the phony knots. On the ceiling, big rectangles of porous cardboard that had perhaps once been white were adorned with damp spots, while the fluorescent tubes were in the process of dying, crackling like insects. It would take a brave customer to leave his clothes, even dirty clothes, on the grimy counter; the few trousers hanging on the metal rack had probably been there for years, abandoned by their owners. Only some stumps of house plants near the window suggested that the business had known better days.

A clerk finally emerged from the gloom at the back of the shop and came up to the counter. Though he wasn't a dwarf, he was a good head shorter than Geneviève, and so ugly that he had only to stand there motionless to blend into the scenery, with which he seemed to be in perfect harmony. He stood planted there, half hidden by the cash register, an antique from before the age of computers, and looked up at Geneviève with a hangdog expression.

"I've come about the ad," she finally stammered.

The man nodded vaguely and looked at the ground, while allowing himself to peer shyly at Geneviève, as if he were studying her bit by bit. You'd think, mused Geneviève, that he was being forced to look at a picture that was both repulsive and fascinating — which she could understand, because she herself was experiencing the same odd mixture of impressions.

They would have spent the rest of the day observing one another if Geneviève hadn't repeated, this time more confidently, that she'd come about the ad. The little fellow, still silent, turned and disappeared into the gloom at the back of the shop.

Had he understood what she'd said? Could he speak and understand French? Could he speak, period? Geneviève was left alone long enough to ask herself dozens of similar questions, and others too, of which the least embarrassing was: Why didn't she run away?

The little man still didn't open his mouth when he finally came back, but with a motion of his head he invited her to follow him to the back of the store. She walked through holding her breath; the smell of Javex and detergents barely masked that of death.

He opened a door at the very back of the room and stepped aside so she could enter a small, windowless bedroom awash with heavy hangings, cushions, and baroque knick-knacks.

A man — or rather, what remained of what must once have been one — was collapsed on a bed made of huge cushions placed directly on the floor. His face was emaciated, the skin wizened and covered with brown spots; while he sometimes managed to whisper two or three words, he had to pay the price in the form of long, cavernous coughing fits.

Laid end to end, his words could be summed up more or less like this: his business had to be sold, fast. His asking price was seventy-five thousand. That would cover the price of the machinery, which was still in good condition. And the buyer would have to respect the lease he'd just signed with the building's owner. The rent was reasonable, and there was a small apartment upstairs. He hadn't been up there for months, as the stairs were too steep. She could sell the furniture, which probably wouldn't be to her taste. The buyer would also have to promise to keep Donald on for at least a year. He was a little odd but he was a good employee, reliable and competent. It was best for him to be confined to the back of the store, though, or he'd drive customers away. If you buy it, he said finally, the customers will come back; you're very pretty.

Geneviève, who'd had plenty of time to observe him during his endless coughing fits, replied that he was very handsome too. It must have been ages since he'd been given a compliment, and he received hers with a strange smile that seemed even more painful than his coughing fits.

§

There was a musty smell in the apartment, but she only had to open the windows to change the air, which was immediately laden with exotic perfumes; the shelf unit in the living-room was overflowing with little pewter or silver knick-knacks in the shape of toads, open hands, or Buddhas, all of which seemed intended to hold sticks or cones of incense. Geneviève would have liked to study the strange collection at greater length, but Donald's gaze, which she could sense on her shoulder, stopped her. Like the clients of Le Pussy, she was content to look at the other components of the bazaar without touching them. The room was overcrowded with easy chairs, with lamps draped in silk scarves, with oriental rugs and cushions, and a multitude of paintings and trinkets.

"I can get rid of them if you want...."

Geneviève, who was looking at the easy chairs, immediately turned to Donald, amazed to finally hear him speak. He was still standing in the doorway, eyes to the ground, as if he were ashamed to hold her gaze.

"A friend of mine would be interested. It isn't suitable for a...a young woman, I don't think.... I hope you aren't offended."

Geneviève refrained from telling him that after working at Le Pussy she wasn't scandalized to see that the designs in the rugs, the lamp bases, the feet and armrests of the easy chairs all depicted phalluses. Those, at least, were well made. But he was right: she'd have to change the furniture. Everything else, though, suited her perfectly: the kitchen, small but spotless; the bedroom, huge and comfortable; the big living-room window that let in the light and looked out on a playground; and finally, the front door, which was completely covered with locks and chains.

"Réjean's always been afraid of burglars," noted Donald, who was dogging her footsteps and anticipating her questions.

"Me too," said Geneviève. "You wouldn't mind too much if I bought this?"

"A little, but I could get used to it. It's hard sometimes, you know, for two people to be cooped up in a small place like this. You're always face to face whether you like it or not. Réjean was pretty hard to take sometimes, and he was so strong, before, anyway.... At least with you there's no danger...."

Geneviève couldn't help completing his sentence to herself: neither one of them ran the slightest risk of being sexually harassed. The thought was so bizarre it was funny.

Since he'd started talking she had seen the odd little man in a different light. His voice was strangely beautiful and deep, with no trace of a lisp or affectation. On the phone, she thought, he must sound very seductive. He was peculiar and evasive, but he seemed harmless. There was even something touching about his name and his ugly duckling's physique.

"Were you...were you fond of Réjean?"

"Before, yes. More than fond. Now, all I feel is pity. That's hard to give and I imagine it's even harder to receive. I'll take care of him till the end, but I'm anxious for him to go, to be perfectly frank.... You should look out the window, it's a quarter to twelve."

Intrigued, Geneviève went over to the big living-room window. The neighbourhood, so quiet till now, suddenly came alive as school was let out. The piercing cries, laughter, and games of children going home for lunch in compact, multicoloured clusters broke off in front of the dry cleaner's. The children detoured around it, nearly running, as if they were afraid a monster would reach out and grab them with a hairy paw. The cries, laughter, and games picked up again a little farther away, but they'd lost some of their brightness.

"Old ladies cross the street too. Some of them even cross themselves. What we need is a new image. It'll take a while, but with you it can be done."

"I've got plenty of time," Geneviève replied.

And she went downstairs immediately with a proposal for Réjean:

"I'll take the apartment but not the furniture, and I give you my word that I'll keep Donald on as long as he wants to stay. In exchange, I'm offering you ten thousand dollars, cash, which I'll bring you within the hour. I'll pay the rest the same way: five thousand a week, cash. Not a word to anybody, though, not even Donald. You'll give me a receipt and that will be that. All right?"

Réjean, who seemed more exhausted than surprised, merely nodded, between two coughing fits.

CHAPTER 11

While Donald was using a week's vacation to settle Réjean into what he euphemistically called a convalescent home, Geneviève was supervising renovations of the business and the apartment, which Donald had cleared of furniture, as promised.

Geneviève enjoyed dealing with the tradesmen. All the electricians, painters, plasterers, and plumbers she convened had entered her store like conquerors, rotating their shoulders, swelling their biceps, and sucking in their bellies while their expert eyes were touching down all over. Brows furrowed, they took notes as if performing complex calculations incomprehensible to ordinary mortals. When the time came to speak, though, they suddenly lost their arrogance. They thought that, to impress their client, they were obliged to puff up their speech as well as their muscles, and they tried to express themselves in that peculiar dialect which the best academics don't always master, even after years of training — the dialect that consists of replacing the simplest words with their most complicated synonyms. Geneviève listened indulgently, the way you listen to strangers who are trying hard to speak your language, and she loved watching their desperate attempts to extricate themselves and to avoid ogling her breasts.

When she told them that she didn't want a written estimate and she was prepared to pay under the table, they heaved a sigh of relief and set to work right away, thrilled that their boss, besides being young and gorgeous, was so accommodating.

However much trouble the men had talking when their hands were empty, they became eloquent when handling their tools; all they needed was time, and something to do. At the start of the day they contented themselves with short, precise, jerky phrases. Why burden themselves with polite chitchat just to ask for the trowel, the screwdriver, or the electrical outlet? After they found what they were looking for, they got down to work, silent and a little gruff, and all you heard were buzzing and pounding and muffled oaths until one of them, who'd found his rhythm, let go and whistled a popular tune or teased one of his colleagues. And then, slowly, as each of the workers adopted the particular cadence of his trade, they'd exchange remarks, comment on the news or weather, or tell stories, always very slowly, not really expecting a response, never taking offence if one of them, concentrating on his work, took refuge in silence. Conversation wasn't the centre of their universe, it was just an accompaniment to their movements, a grace note. First, each of them had to settle into his work and let himself be carried along by its rhythm. After that — and only after that — they could talk.

Geneviève stayed with them as much as possible, asking questions about their trades and doing odd jobs. She knew that this stimulated their zeal, particularly when she bent over to pick up a tool; productivity bonuses never stopped anyone from working. When she sensed that their zeal was stimulated a little too much, she went out shopping in the neighbourhood as Donald had suggested; the owners of the hardware store, the paint store, the restaurant, and the convenience stores would appreciate having as a customer this pretty young woman who never quibbled over prices, paid cash, and didn't ask for a bill.

Spreading the good word, they in turn helped her develop a clientele — as did the owner of the building, to whom she'd paid three months' rent in advance.

When evening came and the workers had left, she shuttled between her old apartment and her new one. There was no question of entrusting her precious cardboard cartons to movers.

In less than a week she'd completed her move and managed to unload the contents of one entire box of bills. She was about to start on a second when doubts assailed her; if she had really launched herself in business and, what was more, taken over a business on the verge of bankruptcy, would she squander her capital so ostentatiously? Wasn't she giving the impression that she had an inexhaustible source of funds, which could only arouse suspicion? Why was she acting like this when she'd always been so prudent? Was she unconsciously trying to get herself arrested?

For a long time she stayed crouched over her cardboard carton, knife in hand, not knowing what to think. Maybe there was a simpler explanation: spending large amounts of money very quickly sometimes brings a sense of euphoria, a feeling of unreality to which she had foolishly succumbed. It was time to come back to earth.

§

"A dry-cleaner's? What do you know about dry-cleaning?"

As Geneviève, dressed in old jeans and a paint-spattered T-shirt, finished cleaning the window, she was observing her father out of the corner of her eye; he stood there in the middle of the room as straight as a fence-post, for fear of soiling his expensive English suit.

"Hardly anything, but I've got a very good, competent employee. I'd like to introduce you but I gave him a few days off while I do some cleaning and tidying. The owner paid for the paint and my friends came and gave me a hand..."

"How much? How much did you pay for this?"

Geneviève could have predicted this: while her mother would have asked who her friends were and what they did, her father wanted numbers, a balance sheet, and profit forecasts. And she'd give them to him. The trick was to talk very fast, to daze him a little, and to answer his questions before he even asked them. That was the only way to deal with a lawyer. In a tone that was steady but firm, and concentrating on her window to avoid meeting his eyes, she spouted the little speech she'd carefully prepared.

"Now listen, Papa; have you ever thought about how much you spend on dry-cleaning every year? Or about all the people who have to have their clothes cleaned, summer and winter? You couldn't dream of a more stable business, one less affected by financial crises. If you want proof, take a look at the classifieds; just try to find a dry-cleaner's for sale. It's true I don't know anything about it, but that doesn't matter; I'm giving myself two years to get this business back on its feet, then I'll sell it and move on to something else. See, what I'm interested in is saving companies. I buy a loser and turn it into a winner. What I buy is some machines and what I sell is growth potential. And this shop meets my expectations on every count: the business is coming apart at the seams because the owner's sick, so it's up to me to pull it back together. And before you ask, I'm telling you right now, no, I don't want any money. This isn't costing me any more than normal rent. I want to prove myself, by myself; why is it you always offer me money?"

Geneviève rather wished that she hadn't concluded like this, but she'd seen her mother do it so often that she couldn't help herself; guilt is something you have to keep alive.

It looked as if the method had worked; while she finished washing the window, she glanced at her father, who seemed to be having trouble swallowing. Maybe she should offer him a glass of water to help him get it down? Yes, that was a good idea. And change the subject before he had time to get back on his feet.

"It's hard for Mama to accept this, I think. I'm starting out in business — in dirty clothes, yet — when she would've liked me to be an artist."

"No, that's not true; she's always been allergic to cleaning products, you know that...."

"Where did she go?"

"Just to get some fresh air. She'll meet us at the restaurant.... Don't worry, I'll try to explain the situation to her. It's not at all foolish, this business.... By the way, while we're alone, I should tell you I ran into Guillaume the other day. He's worried about you..."

"If you see him again, tell him the truth: I've bought a dry-cleaning business. And you'd be doing me a favour if you also told him it's always been my dream to clean dirty clothes. And you can add that I've reached the summit of my ambitions."

"You don't want to see him again, I take it?"

"You got it."

Bernard Vallières may not have been the keenest psychologist the world has ever seen, but he couldn't help thinking that his daughter's tone wouldn't have been so cutting if there hadn't been something to cut. Nor would she have slammed the bathroom door when she went to wash up, leaving him alone in the empty store, still dazed from all these revelations.

Bernard let his gaze wander over the room, first lingering on the cash register, then gliding along the metal rack to the back of the shop where, silhouetted in the shadows, stood some mysterious machines in which he'd gladly have washed his brain. His daughter, his own daughter, was reasoning like a businessman, and wanted to get by completely on her own, without anyone's help, like a real winner.... While he'd been suspecting her of swaying in front of beer-drinkers, or worse, she'd been amassing a little capital, scrutinizing business opportunities, studying markets.... How could he have been so wrong? It was Guillaume who'd put

it into his head, Guillaume and his stories of erotic dancing. Guillaume, who'd been jilted, to put it plainly, had in-
vented all that to get his revenge. A fine hypocrite he was,
behind his innocent appearance. Bernard had always been
sure of that, deep down, despite the sarcasm of Monique,
who kept accusing him of being jealous. The little hypocrite had managed to upset him that day at the restaurant
(never mix business and alcohol, ever). He would phone
the boy, the sooner the better, and that would be the end of
Guillaume, *exit* Guillaume. Game over, Mr. Competitor.

"Ready?"

Bernard was startled to hear his daughter's voice, and
even more surprised at her transformation in such a short
time. She'd traded her jeans, paint-spattered T-shirt, and
the old scarf that held back her hair for a white blouse buttoned to the collar, so spotlessly clean it was dazzling, and
impeccably cut black slacks. Virginal, serious, and totally
irresistible, his little Geneviève, with her head tilted at ten
to twelve as she fastened her earring....

"I know, I look like a lady, but I'll get used to it. You've
got to do what you've got to do when it comes to pleasing
customers. Okay, let's go, Mama will be getting impatient."

§

Geneviève didn't protest when her father paid the bill — a
rather steep one, as a matter of fact. The congratulations
he'd showered on her throughout the meal weren't enough
to express his satisfaction; he still had to pay.

Why refuse him this pleasure? Here was one person at
least, whom she had eating out of her hand. There would
always be time to curb his enthusiasm if he started trying
to give her advice.

Her mother's attitude, on the other hand, worried her
a little. She hadn't said a word throughout the meal and
she'd drunk more wine than usual, and she seemed slightly
tipsy. She was twisting strands of hair around her fingers,

at the risk of taking the curl out. The elegant suit, the jewels, the blusher, the eye-shadow.... Her mother was still impeccably turned out, still perfect, without the slightest crack, still just as wonderfully superficial, but now she'd drunk a little too much wine and she seemed unsteady, as if she had run down. Geneviève felt like shaking her to get her ticking again.

"You know, Geneviève," she finally let drop half-heartedly, when dessert had been served, "the only thing I care about is your happiness...."

She'd taken her time, but at least it proved that her psychologist-mother's batteries weren't completely dead.

CHAPTER 12

Guillaume had let himself be dragged along to a pub near the university, but he'd left the group of students and professors in mid-libation. He didn't tolerate alcohol well, and tolerated even less their laughter and backslapping, not to mention Stéphanie, who'd been hovering around him for a while now. How can you tell such a nice girl that you don't feel like being consoled?

Pierced by the cold wind, he pulled up the hood of his parka and set off for the nearest Metro station. The city sidewalks were so icy that he had to shuffle like a cross-country skier and keep his eyes on the ground. The task was all the more arduous because he was still in an alcoholic daze, so he had a hard time reaching the door of the station, where another trial awaited. Because of some phenomenon of physics that he'd never understood, everything inside the tunnels seemed stuck to the door, making it impossible to open it without also dragging along a tremendous mass of warm air, thousands of passengers, and the odd subway car.

While he waited for some Hercules at the other end of the system to get a door open, thereby equalizing the pressure, he looked up at a strange illuminated sign on the other side of the street. A host of flashing bulbs, forming a gigantic

V whose arms soared towards the sky, tried to catch the attention of passersby, to no avail; the pedestrians walked with their heads down and their coat collars pulled up — as if, to prevent themselves from looking, they'd decided to wear blinkers. No one but Guillaume saw those yellow bulbs that, in a pinch, might suggest a flight of wild geese. It took him a moment to grasp the fact that the two arms of the V represented the legs of a woman who, for some inexplicable reason, was hanging upside down.

It was a fascinating image: all these tiny passersby, wrapped in their coats and trudging along, their eyes glued to the toes of their boots, seeing nothing of those enormous legs that seemed lit up for the sole purpose of attracting his gaze. He crossed the street without thinking, and looked at the menu this business offered to prospective clients: 24 *filles* girls 24 *heures* hours.

There wasn't a chance in a thousand that Geneviève was one of those two dozen *vivantes* live *filles* girls who were dancing for an audience of old *cochons* pigs, but it didn't cost anything to go and check one more time. What else could he do, still half-drunk in the middle of the afternoon? And so he pushed the door — which opened without offering the slightest resistance — and immediately found himself in the heart of the jungle.

Mind you, it would take a lot of imagination to transform the plastic palm trees into a tropical forest, the tedious rock music into African drums, and the smell of beer and cigarettes into the perfumes of exotic flowers; but the stifling heat had been imitated so convincingly that Guillaume would surely have suffocated had a kind young woman not rushed up to help him out of his coat. Clad in a simple synthetic leopard skin cut to enhance her protuberances, which were nicely rounded, the young woman asked him, as naturally as you can imagine, which he preferred — the waterfall or the lianas.

"I...I don't know," Guillaume stammered, still dazed and not absolutely sure he'd understood what this high-heeled Jane had asked him. "It's the first time I've been here..."

"You should start with the waterfall."

The waterfall? The thought that a cascade of water could flow right here in the city, and in the heart of winter, seemed so absurd that the word itself sounded strange. All things considered, though, her suggestion sounded more sensible than the lianas, and he nodded his consent. Jane rolled away — no other verb could describe her gait — and Guillaume tried to follow her through a maze of corridors, chairs, and tables. As his eyes weren't accustomed to the darkness yet, he had to keep them glued to Jane's ass so he wouldn't get lost, and there was something hypnotic about the spectacle of her swaying rear end.

After pushing open the saloon-type swinging doors, they entered a huge room half-filled with clients who were silently watching the back wall, where, between artificial rocks and a scattering of green plants, a thin thread of water flowed down into a bubble bath. Two bathers, entirely naked, seemed to be enjoying soaping one another.

"There are booths in the back," said Jane, pulling up a chair.

Still in a state of hypnosis, Guillaume sat down facing the waterfall, but Jane promptly stepped in and blocked his view. She leaned slowly towards the table, as if she wanted to place her breasts there, and, looking him squarely in the eyes, asked if there was anything he wanted.

"A beer, please."

"You have to ask a waitress. I'm an usherette."

Though she had seemed downright winsome before, Jane now showed herself to be a grouch, but there she stayed, right in front of him, preventing him from admiring the show. She had to repeat that she was an *usherette*, in a tone that had nothing pleasant about it, before Guillaume finally understood what she was waiting for; he opened his wallet and held out a five-dollar bill. Immediately Jane's smile came back, and she favoured him with a suggestive pout before turning and walking away, hips swaying. To judge by her reaction, the tip had been adequate.

He wasn't the only one to pick up the signal, it seemed; before he even had time to put away his wallet, a waitress in a minimal bathing-suit came to prevent him once again from admiring the water nymphs' show. He had to buy a three-dollar beer to finally get some peace. At that price, thought Guillaume, a movie was a better deal; there were more spectators to share the cost of the scenery.

The two women, probably deciding they were clean enough, had stepped out of the water and were now towelling each other dry while spectators tossed coins into the pool. Immediately another waitress took over, and washed herself on her own, which didn't seem to disappoint the crowd; while the two previous bathers had small breasts, this one's were enormous. Erotic shows sometimes offer strange equivalences.

Guillaume sipped his beer and tried to relax. After all, it would be silly to deprive himself of a show that had already cost him so much. So he gazed at the girl who was slowly soaping her breasts and buttocks, and he reacted just as he usually did when he came across off-the-rack fantasies. At times like this, his brain seemed to be divided into two perfectly watertight zones. If he kept his eyes wide open for a while, all words and ideas disappeared, replaced by images, and he entered a world of dreams where everything became possible. If he could keep himself in this state for more than a minute, he'd have a cumbersome erection to deal with. Then he only had to blink and the gate to the other zone — the zone of words and ideas — would pop open. Every time he leafed through *Playboy* or rented porn videos with his Friday-night friends, the same cold-shower phenomenon took place. Just one blink, like the film director's clapper, transformed the images into what they really were: the gorgeous girl with the come-hither smile was just a photo on glossy paper, a touched-up photo of an actress who'd been made up for hours and had suffered the lighting and the volley of flashes to get her hands on a cheque. All things considered, he preferred the little movies his own imagination screened for him in bed at night. They were free, and the scripts were a lot more imaginative.

He'd been faithful to his habits that day, first letting himself be pervaded by the images (his hands approaching the bather's breasts, weighing them, touching them, soaping and caressing them), then jumping into the zone of words (did the young woman know about the class-action suit against breast implant manufacturers?) Then he'd entered a third zone, where images and words were inextricably mingled; the anonymous bather had suddenly taken on the features of Geneviève, and she'd left her bubble bath for a young girl's bedroom, where she'd peeled off her jeans and T-shirt for the first time. Geneviève, whom he'd subsequently undressed so often, was now in this bath of foam, caressing her breasts and giving hard-ons to several dozen beer drinkers.

Unable to take any more, Guillaume looked away at the audience, made up of members of a Golden Age club and a few younger men: executives on the make, credit union managers, university professors, and computer nerds. All were gazing at the breasts of the bather, who stroked herself again and again, trying to forget all these eyes clinging to her like grubby hands.

Most of the customers stayed slumped in their seats, stupefied, but others were getting up and lumbering to one of the booths at the back of the room, where they could shut themselves away to find relief. Guillaume couldn't swear to it, but he thought some of them didn't hesitate to enter a booth that was already occupied, and a fair number had their eyes on him when he got up to head for the liana room.

Here the set depicted another plastic jungle, where girls descended from the ceiling, clutching gymnasts' cables that stood in for lianas, to grab the bills customers left on the tables. Depending on the amount, most likely, they would sometimes hang around for a few moments, or climb right back up in search of another bill, as if they were characters from a video game in search of an outside life.

He'd had more than enough. During the two weeks that he'd been going to places like this, the same thoughts had kept running through his head, in the same order, and he hadn't had the slightest success. The thought of Geneviève plying such a trade shocked him but, strangely enough, it aroused him too; it made her more mysterious, even admirable in a way: you had to be brave to take off your clothes like that. She was brave, while he had never felt like such a coward. Why was he wasting his time pacing city and suburbs to visit places like this, why was he spending a fortune, when all he had to do was swallow his pride and finish off what he'd started. He hadn't hesitated to walk through the neighbourhood where Geneviève lived, in the hope of running into her, so why not just post himself outside her place, even if it meant freezing for a few hours? Simply tailing her would let him shake off the doubts he'd been keeping alive for so long. What did he have to lose, when you got right down to it, except whatever pride he still had? And if ever his suspicions were confirmed, it would be painful, of course, but maybe he'd finally be able to forget her. And if all these scenarios were nothing but a construction of idiotic hypotheses, wouldn't that be even more painful? No matter, his mind was made up.

And so he emerged from the jungle, walked resolutely on the icy sidewalk at the risk of a broken leg, opened the door of the Metro station without the slightest difficulty, and went directly to the building where he had lived with Geneviève.

Why should he cool his heels when all he needed was to boot himself in the rear once and for all, and go and knock on her door? He rang the bell for apartment 605 and, getting no response, pressed the button again, for a very long time, with no more success. Then a delivery man came out and Guillaume was able to slip inside the lobby, where a miniature fountain flowed amid green plants; it had never seemed so ridiculous. He'd moved from one jungle to another, but he was in no mood to think about coincidences, let alone the appropriateness of what he was doing; why was he so determined to knock on a door that he couldn't open because he no longer had the key? He wasn't going to force it, after all. Was he going to sit in the corridor and wait for Geneviève to come home?

He got his answer when the elevator left him in front of the wide-open door to apartment 605. All the furniture was gone, and the empty apartment held only canvas dropcloths covering the floor, along with ladders, paint cans, and the rest of a painter's paraphernalia.

The janitor, whom he'd obviously disturbed in the middle of lunch, delivered the final blow when he told him that Geneviève had paid the regulation three months' rent in cash, and that she hadn't left a forwarding address.

CHAPTER 13

Brodeur was watching the dancer at the San Francisco and
doing his best to look disillusioned — it was the best way
to hide his desire, he thought. How could he not respond
to this show, he who'd gone without for months? And since
it was his job that had brought him here, why not stay a
little longer than he had to, at least it gave him something
else to think about? All right, so his doctor had advised
him to cut down on coffee and alcohol, but had he ever
mentioned that getting an eyeful could have any effect on
his ulcers?

So he admired the dancer till the end of her act — which
was much too brief for his liking — but he had a hard time
watching the one who came next. Her breasts were nice,
her movements weren't lacking in grace, and she discharged
her task conscientiously, but Brodeur looked away, a little
uncomfortable, while he waited for Nathalie — who was
calling herself Sandra now — to finish her show. As long as
it was a stranger it was easy enough to let your imagination run wild, but some memories you'd rather not activate. And there'd been a time when Nathalie was much
more than an informer.

While waiting for her to finish her act, he studied his
glass, thinking of the unexpected turn his investigation had

taken. A good thing there was work, sometimes, so you could forget about the rest.

It had all started with a modern version of a bottle cast into the ocean. The message he'd typed on his computer keyboard had drifted in space for a few microseconds, bounced off a satellite antenna, and finally come to rest in some hundreds of cathode tubes scattered over hundreds of police stations: anyone who'd heard anything at all about the theft or loss of two sticks of dynamite was requested to communicate with Lieutenant Brodeur of the crimes against property division, Sûreté du Québec.

A few weeks later, some colleagues in Laval had arrested one Robert "Snake" Thériault, who was believed to be associated with the Hell's Angels — this hadn't been proved yet — and was suspected of supplying anything to anybody, on demand, and then bragging about it quite openly; in less than thirty minutes he could deliver, like so much pizza, any reasonable quantity of drugs, firearms, or munitions. Had the cops not stopped his trafficking by setting the trap he'd just fallen into, he could have published a catalogue. A simple search of his residence, which he used as a warehouse, had let them pile up enough evidence to fill a medium-sized courtroom, provided that they handled it with the greatest caution — otherwise the courthouse would have been blown to bits.

One of these policemen had remembered Brodeur's message and immediately sent him a fax that summed up the case. No one had stepped forward to post his bail, so Thériault could be interrogated in all tranquillity. Brodeur showed up at once.

Like most of his colleagues, Brodeur conducted his interrogations with a scrupulous respect for his profession's code of ethics. A prisoner, even one who represents the dregs of society, is still a human being and consequently enjoys an incalculable number of rights. For instance, no one can use him as a guinea pig to confirm the old theory, inspired by acupuncture, that a knee in the balls can sometimes have a miraculous effect on memory problems. A careful reading of the code of ethics could turn up some grey zones, however. For instance, the notion of a human being was never clearly defined, so you could reasonably wonder if a suspect who didn't answer your questions quickly and politely, whose memory was as flawed as Richard Nixon's, and who had, to be blunt, excluded himself from the human race through his behaviour or attitude, could claim to enjoy the rights that had been set out — and this, obviously, was the spirit of the law — with a view to protecting honest citizens. Nothing then expressly prohibited inadvertently applying a knee to their parts.

Once he'd revealed his methods of interrogation, Brodeur had had no trouble making Thériault admit that some time in November he'd sold two sticks of dynamite — not one or three or four, but precisely two sticks; Brodeur was jubilant — to a young woman (Thériault actually used a much more vulgar expression) who wore dark glasses and a very long coat. And that was all he knew: it was dark, it was a long time ago, she'd come into the bar, asked for the dynamite, gone with him to the parking lot, where he'd handed over the goods, then she'd left and that was that.

Brodeur was convinced that Thériault had told him the naked truth. The young woman certainly hadn't left her calling card, and it was miracle enough that he even remembered her. But the policeman couldn't resign himself to abandoning such a promising piece of information without trying to squeeze out all the sap, so he resorted to a method that, while less striking, was nonetheless, in his experience, terribly effective. To activate the memory of Thériault, who smoked like a chimney, he sent him back to his cell and saw to it that he had no cigarettes for the rest of the day. When Brodeur turned up the next morning to resume his interrogation, he offered him a coffee and an enormous muffin packed with chocolate chips and then, on the corner of the table, placed — well within sight, but out of reach — a pack of Thériault's brand of cigarettes.

If, in the eyes of certain specialists, the absorption of nicotine entails a loss of memory, the promise of nicotine, on the other hand, seems to restore the damaged circuits instantly. Eyes glued to the cigarette Brodeur had lit, Thériault made a prodigious effort to recall the most minute details of the matter he was interested in: the young woman was alone; she'd probably come by car but he hadn't noticed the make or colour; she had long, curly, flaming red hair and a mole on her cheek; he hadn't seen her eyes because of the dark glasses; she stood about one metre sixty; she hadn't taken off her coat but she looked as if she was stacked — in fact, he'd told her that with her equipment she didn't need dynamite to earn her living, and she'd replied that she was well aware of that. She had some kind of an accent, not exactly French from France but something like it. Afterwards she paid and she left and that's all, I swear that's all, now can I have a cigarette?

Brodeur had thanked him for his valuable co-operation by leaving him the package; then he had gone out to get some air and breathe it in deeply. Never had an interrogation been so difficult; while Thériault was greedily eyeing the cigarettes, Brodeur had been ogling the large-size coffee, whose aroma had filled the whole room.

The computer obviously couldn't make use of the association young *redhead/stacked/dynamite*, but a weird idea had crossed Brodeur's mind while he was tapping away; he'd thought about a sentence he'd scornfully jotted on a scrap of paper: *The suspect is a male.* Now it appeared that he had to correct it: the suspect *may be* a male. That was even more absurd, if he thought about it, but it was possible all the same, at least theoretically, for the suspect to be a woman. A lone woman who'd planned and executed a bank heist, without an accomplice and without a word to anyone.... Could the woman be an accomplice, who had simply bought the dynamite and obediently handed it over to her boyfriend, who was waiting in the car? An accomplice who was stacked, who didn't need dynamite to make her living and was *well aware of it*, and who could therefore be a dancer or something like that?

The trail couldn't have been more flimsy, but still, Brodeur had launched another bottle into the sea: *dynamite, sand, dancer*. If that means anything to you, contact Lieutenant Brodeur, crimes against property division, Sûreté du Québec. The only responses had been a lot of jokes in very bad taste, and the names of a few dancers who were known to be reliable informers. Among these was Nathalie, who was now working at the San Francisco; was it worth bothering her for so little? Did he really need a pretext for going to see the girls dance? And what should he say to her?

"A girl who's come into a lot of money recently?"

She would have gone on a trip or bought herself a sports car, something along those lines? No, nothing comes to mind. There're so many girls nowadays.... And by the way, don't you notice anything?

Nathalie, who was back in her waitress's outfit and standing at his side, was offering herself to his gaze, smiling, one hand on her hip, while Brodeur racked his brain to come up with an answer to this horrible question that seemed, every time it was asked, to completely annihilate his faculties of observation. If a colleague had shaved his moustache, Brodeur would compliment him on his new glasses. And what can you say to a woman who asks you this question, while sparing her sensitivity? How had she changed, exactly? Put on weight? Had a root canal? Broken a fingernail? Plucked her moustache?

"Look higher...."

"Your hair?" (Given the way she was dressed, it was easy to proceed by elimination.)

"I've got blonde streaks. They look good, don't they?"

"They're great. Make you look younger."

"Thanks. So you're looking for a girl who might have come into some money. Is that all? Don't you know anything else?"

"There's no dope involved. And she's got some kind of

an accent."

"What does that mean, some kind of an accent? What kind?"

"Well, not French, but something like it. I don't know exactly what that means.... Let me know if you hear anything, okay?"

"All right, *lieutenant*."

"Thank you, *mademoiselle*."

Brodeur watched Nathalie walk away towards another table, and thought about the minuscule thread that was supposed to link Mademoiselle Nathalie, Lieutenant Brodeur, and a bank heist in the Laurentians. A minuscule thread, an idiotic argument, but one that he'd follow all the same, in his spare time. The suspect, whoever he or she was, would spend the money sooner or later.

Then he watched the show, thinking that the girls in this line of work were paid well; nobody forced them to do it, and it was no more degrading than selling heat pumps.

The words were gradually erased and all he could see were images — beautiful, disconcerting images that he gazed at for a long time, feeling a little sad.

§

In the very first sequence of the film, entitled *Sandy and Her Friends*, the heroine had already exhausted the resources of her imagination to satisfy her partner, whose name was Bart, but the best was yet to come: Bart's friends would soon be joining them for a little party during which Sandy would simultaneously bring to orgasm five young men at the peak of their power. The suspense, of course, was unbearable.

Raphaël, Francis, and Alexandre had thought they were doing the right thing by reproducing the Friday-night ritual in every detail: the beer, the four lines of coke, the pool, and finally, to wrap it up with a flourish, one of the tapes Francis swiped from his father's collection, which usually brought on torrents of laughter. It was, they thought, an excellent way to celebrate the return of the prodigal son. If Sandy's performance couldn't cheer up Guillaume, nothing could. And anyway, it was better than hearing him ask how he could have lived for so long with a girl whose only ambition was to press trousers.

But the beer, the dope, and the pool hadn't freed Guillaume of his obsession: Geneviève had bought a dry-cleaner's. Geneviève, his Geneviève, had become a dry-cleaner. She spent her days washing shirts and pressing pants, and seemed very happy with her situation. Does that make sense to you? Geneviève? A *dry-cleaner?* What's the point?

"Drop it, man, watch the movie. That'll take your mind off her."

Guillaume couldn't. He was still thinking about the call he'd received from Geneviève's father. Why had her father treated him so curtly when just a few days earlier he'd readily shared such amazing confidences? And how could you explain a man who'd seemed overcome with admiration for his daughter accepting this as the peak of her ambition? No doubt he'd been wrong to think that Geneviève made her living like Sandy, but it was even harder to admit that she'd become a dry-cleaner. Why not a cleaning lady, while she was at it?

His friends might be right: he shouldn't have got so attached to Geneviève, he should have been like them and just enjoyed life. Taken advantage of his parents' money, grabbed everything that came his way, and not asked himself too many questions; there'd always be time to imprison himself....

Francis was thinking about Geneviève too — wondering what she was like in bed. If she'd managed to entangle Guillaume so badly, despite her total lack of conversation, she must have some qualities.... Why shouldn't he indulge himself with her, now that she was officially free? He'd have to let things settle down for Guillaume, and then a few weeks later he'd find himself in bed with her and he'd take care of her like Sandy's friends.... Francis felt the onset of an erection he had difficulty suppressing. He watched the rest of the film totally motionless, for fear that his friends would laugh at him if they saw him wriggling in his chair. Try as he might to think about something else, he couldn't do it; this was the first time in his life that he'd been turned on by a porn film. Was he getting old?

Raphaël thought about Christ, who had come to earth to redeem the sins of the world, and about Geneviève, who was going to cloister herself in a little shop and clean other people's dirty clothes. Maybe the religious hypothesis wasn't so dumb after all. They were there, the four of them, watching a porn film as they'd done so many times before. Just for laughs, of course, not taking it seriously. They always used a torrent of words to mask their guilt, though it didn't stop them from shamelessly watching a girl who was doing everything possible to infect herself with the AIDS virus. Who knew if Geneviève, perhaps unconsciously, wasn't right? Even in strictly financial terms, it was far from stupid: her little business would let her live peacefully, without beating her brains out, while they were breaking their butts racking up degrees with no idea what they'd find at the end of the trail....

Only Alex was really watching the film, and he'd have had to be tortured to confess what was on his mind. It wasn't so much his erection that was troubling him — he was used to them — as the way it had appeared. Once every now and then was no cause for concern; all men had such fantasies, apparently. But it had become a regular pattern, and obsessive: to get turned on, he had to identify with Sandy.

A few beers, four lines of coke, some pool, and a porn film. The recipe, though infallible, hadn't worked the way they'd wanted. Oh, there'd been a few jokes at the start of the film, but the retorts had been brief and the laughter subdued. The four young men had watched the rest of Sandy's performance in silence, as if they were ancient men of forty. They had grown old, all of them, at the same time.

CHAPTER 14

"What about sex? Don't you miss it sometimes?"

Geneviève had lifted the heavy iron, which was held in place by a system of springs and pulleys, and she took the time to move it away before sending a stunned look at Donald, who was preparing to drop a pile of white shirts into the washing machine. Donald wanted to die; instead of thinking first and talking after, he'd blurted out the question, as if Geneviève weren't his boss and even, to be honest, as if she weren't a woman.

Thanks to the few crumbs of information she'd let him pick up, he'd finally realized that she'd been living with a young man for a while, that their affair was over, and that no one had taken his place. "What about sex? Don't you miss it sometimes?" No sooner did the question cross his mind than the words were out of his mouth. God Almighty, what had got into him? Uneasy, he filled the compartment with detergent and closed the lid of the machine. When he finally turned towards Geneviève, he saw her shrug and pick up the iron again, heaving a strange sigh that merged with a burst of steam. This was most likely the only answer he would get. It was just as well.

Wouldn't he have reacted the same way if she had asked him the same question? Donald thought about Réjean while he was sorting the clothes for the next load: Réjean, who was constantly asking, between coughing fits, for a glass of water, or some aspirins, or a new magazine, or anything else. Even when Réjean was at the very back of the shop and couldn't see Donald, he was guided by an infallible talent for making the most eccentric requests at the worst moments. Donald only had to be busy pressing a very expensive dress or dealing with a customer and the sinister groan would resonate — Donald, bring me this, Donald, bring me that — and Donald would abandon the customer, who would take to his heels. Réjean had never found pleasure except in domination, a characteristic aggravated by his illness; he would have liked to contaminate the entire world, destroy everything around him, beginning with what he held dearest. Even today, when Donald went to visit him after work, he insisted on being satisfied, though every effort failed. Now that he could no longer use brute force, he had found another, equally violent way to achieve his goals: "You don't love me, Donald, you've never loved me, and you're using the fact that I'm on my deathbed to get your revenge, after everything I've done for you...." *After everything I've done for you*, yes, he'd actually dared to say that — he whom Donald had had to approach on bended knee to collect his salary. If Geneviève had asked him the same question, he'd have heaved a big sigh. And he hoped Réjean would heave a big sigh too, a final big sigh, but Réjean would end his life like everything else, with every effort failing.

It was strange that Réjean had always neglected his business, whereas his apartment was meticulously kept up. Perhaps he thought there was a municipal bylaw stating that dry-cleaners had to be poorly maintained. Or that customers would think their clothes looked cleaner in contrast. Perhaps too there was another explanation, in keeping with his deepest nature. While in his private life Réjean made a show of accepting his homosexuality, he'd always been ashamed of it in public, never wanting to admit that he and Donald were one of the most long-standing couples in the community. Not once in their twenty years together had they gone out in public, even to the movies, and Réjean had always refused to live with Donald: if we had the same address people would talk, it could hurt business, we have to keep up appearances, you understand....

As for Geneviève, she didn't seem to have a private life. Her work was her life.

What on earth had got into him, daring to ask her about sex?

Donald put both hands on the machine and felt the vibrations spread from his arms to his legs. While this exercise didn't give him any new thoughts, at least it shook up the old ones. He ventured a furtive glance; she was busy pressing clothes. And she didn't seem angry; instead, she seemed lost in thought, as so often happens when you're sliding an iron across a jacket, very gently, with a little movement of the wrist to avoid the buttons, like that, yes.... She wasn't an expert yet, of course, but you couldn't deny that she had a certain knack — and tenacity, too. He never would have thought she'd be able to take it for so long. It was three months now that she'd been learning the trade and plaguing him with questions, as if she really wanted to learn, as if she really appreciated his work. But she was a strange girl, all the same.

At first he'd thought it was a just a whim, a passing fancy for a young girl from a good family who wanted to prove to Daddy that she knew how to run a business while she waited to succeed him as head of the family firm. "Lend me a hundred thousand dollars, Papa, and I'll show you what I can do." How else to explain a girl like her, from a wealthy family, who'd gone to private schools and still had the accent, buying a dry-cleaner's? It wouldn't last; one of these days her father's capital, and his patience, would run out; she would quickly learn that you didn't become a dry-cleaner overnight, and that it wasn't so easy to build up a clientele.

Still, Donald had decided to work for her, out of simple curiosity but also because he didn't have the heart to look for another job.

To his amazement, Geneviève always paid his salary cash on the nail, despite the long hours they spent doing nothing while waiting for the customers to come back. She'd even given him, without his asking for it, the raise that Réjean had always refused: "You aren't just my employee, Monsieur Donald, you're my teacher too." That was sheer flattery, but he went along with it, and taught her the principles of the trade on some old clothes from the Salvation Army.

And then it was spring, a spring made to order for dry-cleaners, featuring rain, storms, blizzards, a two-day heat wave and then another blizzard, as if the good Lord had gone crazy and was amusing Himself for a week by organizing a potpourri of all the seasons. The customers went crazy too: they would bring in their salt-stained winter coats and the spring clothes they wanted freshened up, insisting that everything be cleaned while they waited because they had nothing left to wear. Under such circumstances even the most incompetent dry-cleaners would have found customers, but Réjean probably would have taken the opportunity to head for ruin: he'd have asked for a chaise longue set up near the window on the pretext of enjoying the sun, and then he'd have been stricken with a violent coughing fit whenever a customer came in.

There was no question that Geneviève was a much prettier sight, but you had to look elsewhere to explain her success. She had managed to win back the clientele very gently, without any fuss, by thinking of all sorts of insignificant details that added up to something fine, something really fine.

First she tried to erase the memory of Réjean by displaying the shop's new colours. Rather than sticking with the orange letters on a black background, which were visible for kilometres but gave you a headache as soon as you looked at them up close, she'd chosen to make her own sign, after going through a good many sketches and jars of paint. The result was no great work of art — far from it — but its awkward side was precisely what attracted people. Passersby had to stand close to the window to read the message, which let them see not only that the business had a new owner, but also that the walls had been repainted and the ceiling repaired. And while the neon sign still didn't work, it was so well polished that it seemed luminous again.

Geneviève had spent a lot on her housecleaning, and the investment soon paid dividends. Children no longer took detours, and the customers who dared to step inside were greeted by the sound of little bells instead of an ugly electric buzzer. The customers, she told herself, didn't have to feel like rats that had lost their way in a labyrinth. Greeted by tinkling bells, they were well disposed to listen to the strange music coming from speakers set into the walls. It was never rock, which would have upset the elderly, nor was it French ballads from the sixties, which would have horrified the younger clientele. Geneviève preferred classical music, and seemed partial to solos for cello, violin or piano, as if she couldn't tolerate a mixture of instruments.

And the dish of candies that sat permanently on the counter, dipped into by children and old ladies who were delighted to be offered a little treat; and the ferns in the window; and the incense she sometimes burned, or the dried leaves she wet down with a drop of oil every day to revive their perfumes (more than the decor or the music, Geneviève liked to perfect the odours); and the tactic — more openly commercial, but one that she was smart enough not to overdo — of making customers think she'd found a ten-dollar bill in an inside coat pocket: "No, you don't owe me a thing, I'm the one who owes you." It didn't cost a lot to build up a team of zealous advertising agents who were quick to spread the word of her unfailing honesty through the neighbourhood.

Donald had added some little details too, suggesting

to Geneviève that she wear wide-legged black slacks and a white blouse buttoned to the neck. Though impractical (she was constantly using the lint brush), these clothes helped make her look older (which she accepted graciously — of course she was young!), thereby adding to her credibility. But even if she hid her figure, avoided any trace of makeup, and wore her hair like an old schoolmistress, she was never able to transform herself into an austere young woman. She was still desirable, at least to those who like those kind of curves; the first customers, in fact, were the local machos, who came strutting in rotating their shoulders. Geneviève always treated them curtly but correctly, never joining in their game. God only knew if she'd have been able to profit from it; after all, if there are restaurants where sexy wait-resses offer their customers the sight of bare breasts along with the fried eggs, why not a sexy dry-cleaner?

It was a joke, of course, just a joke, in questionable taste maybe, that Donald had made one day when they still barely knew one another. She didn't appreciate it. Not at all. She stayed in a bad mood for days, though he apolo-gized effusively. Since then, he hadn't dared make the slight-est insinuation, even remotely. And now, three months later, he'd allowed himself to ask her if she missed sex. How, for God's sake, could he have let himself do that?

There's nothing worse than trying to avoid a subject. You end up obsessed by it, inevitably putting your foot in it, as if your mind is rebelling against being censored. How could someone so young and so pretty spend her life clean-ing other people's clothes, and then shut herself up inside her apartment like a cloistered nun, never going to the movies or a restaurant? It had to prey on her, didn't it? Didn't Réjean, who'd had a taste of it, like to repeat that women didn't really enjoy sex? Maybe he was right after all.

§

Geneviève was so afraid that Donald might suffer from the horrible propensity of some homosexuals to relate everything to sex that she'd made him understand very clearly, from the outset, that she wouldn't tolerate any allusion to the subject. Maybe her reaction had been a little abrupt, but the message had registered; when they played Scrabble while waiting for customers, Donald would lose the game rather than put down the word "sex."

They'd never fallen into the trap of sharing confidences. Condemned to close quarters, they quickly sensed that it was better to avoid recounting the stories of their lives, so they stuck to agreeably superficial conversation, never straying from a certain formality. By choosing darkness over harsh lighting and silence over long sentences, they got to know each other slowly, without haste, and without even realizing it.

Geneviève enjoyed this way of getting acquainted; among other advantages, it kept her mind pleasantly occupied while her body was mobilized to perform repetitive tasks. Each little remark dropped by Donald, his most innocent acts, his smallest quirks, even, became so many clues to be decoded and interpreted. Donald had an odd way of pressing pants, doing it gently in the morning and more and more violently as the day wore on. During the last hour he sometimes turned up the heat of the iron and lingered a little too long on the crotch, as if he wanted to burn it. She guessed then that he was thinking about Réjean, whom he'd soon be visiting after work, as he did every evening. Driven by a strange selflessness, he would offer him reading and conversation, then feed him with a spoon. The next day he would clean his newly stained clothes and grumble about babies' nasty habit of spitting up their food.

Why should they need to share confidences when they only had to observe and interpret? Perhaps couples should operate that way, she often thought; since by nature they were condemned to a lack of privacy, they should avoid sharing confidences, flee dialogue like the plague, and learn how to *not* communicate, so that married life could become as fascinating as a murder mystery.

And what about sex? Don't you miss it sometimes? The question was so crude that at first Geneviève was startled, but she quickly forgave Donald his indiscretion. When she turned to him, he blushed to his ears and assumed his hangdog look. The remark had got away from him, that was all, there was no reason to make a fuss over it, and it had just confirmed what she'd always suspected: when he wasn't thinking about Réjean, Donald was observing her. He was trying to decode her, to understand her. It would be inappropriate for her to take offence — after all, she did the same thing. He was wondering about her sex life? As long as it was matters like that he was pondering, she had nothing to worry about.

Was he expecting an answer? Surely not. They'd managed to say nothing to each other during the long winter months, when they had all the time in the world to talk, so they would go on saying nothing in the spring, now that the customers had come back. Their conversations, still just as superficial, were constantly interrupted by the needs of the job, and it often happened that a question asked in the morning wouldn't get answered till evening, at closing time, or even the next day — as if their work had been merely a long digression — or never: the question would stay suspended in the air, like fragments of cotton or flannel, eventually dissolving in the Javex fumes.

What about sex? Don't you miss it sometimes? It takes a lot more than shrugs and Javex fumes to make a question like that disappear, one that clings to your mind like a spot of tar to a shirt. Rub it with a turpentine-soaked rag, and all you get is a spot that's slightly paler but keeps spreading.

And what about sex? During the winter months she'd had far too much to do even to think about it. She'd had to move, get to know her customers, learn how to deal with the bank manager, pay for permits and taxes, as well as pick up a trade that was a lot more complicated than she'd imagined. With the best teacher in the world, it had taken her more than a month to become a decent presser, and even now she handled only the simplest garments made of the most common fabrics. In spite of all the questions she'd asked Donald, she still knew practically nothing about cleaning, which requires long experience and a solid knowledge of chemistry. She had also studied business accounting, about which she'd known absolutely nothing. Every evening she shut herself away in her apartment to bone up on manuals and do exercises until she was dropping with fatigue. And sex? Sorry, no time to think about that.

It was only when she'd acquired a certain skill at pressing that her mind had been able to run free. And then, on occasion, she would think about sex, yes, while the iron was gliding over the cloth. Odd ideas would crop up, as if they'd been hidden in a wrinkle or under the flap of a pocket. Fleeting ideas, ephemeral images that presented themselves at the worst moments, like those strange urges to sneeze that always wait till both your hands are busy. When she was observing Donald, for instance, and wondering what he'd been up to with Réjean, and by what miracle he hadn't been infected. Or when customers brought in clothes that reminded her of Danièle's nurse's uniform, Tao's kimono, or the gymnast's gear of a girl called Roxane. It wasn't all that long ago; it was so near and at the same time so far — in another world, another life — and anyway it was other people's sex lives, not hers.

"Know what, Donald?"

With his hand on the doorknob, Donald had his end-of-day hangdog look. She didn't have to say much to him at these moments to keep him there a while longer.

"Do you need a hand?"

"No, it's not that. I just wanted to tell you that I've been thinking about what you asked me this morning."

"I hope you'll accept my apology, I honestly don't know what got into me..."

"That's all right. I just wanted to tell you I don't miss it.

I'm getting my virginity back."

"You don't have to..."

"I know. That's why I wanted to answer your question. Bye now, and be brave."

§

Geneviève thought about Donald's question again that evening, when she went upstairs to her apartment. Stretched out comfortably on the sofa, she allowed herself to dream while she listened to music, and those dreams took her so far that she caught herself unbuttoning her slacks and letting her hand glide slowly as far as her panties. If it's true that need creates the organ, is it possible that the absence of need.... She stopped her hand midway, suddenly aware of how ridiculous the situation was. Even in her early adolescence she'd never felt her hymen. So how could she expect to know if it had grown back?

CHAPTER 15

The highway was empty on this Sunday afternoon in June, and the pavement was perfectly dry, but Geneviève persisted in driving in the right-hand lane, at a speed that rarely exceeded eighty kilometres an hour. She hadn't driven her car for so long that she had to think before doing each of those little things that had once seemed so natural. With her hands clutching the wheel, she kept her eyes glued to the road, never looking in the rearview mirror for fear of seeing another one of those maniacs tapping his temple with his index finger. She'd see him a few moments later anyway, after he'd passed her, gesturing with his middle finger. Sometimes, if an automobile was filled with kids, the youngsters would turn around to face her and copy their father's moves. Well-behaved little children, introduced when still very young to speed, performance, productivity, and competitiveness — the barbaric word that's always accompanied by a swagger, and pride at being able to pronounce all those syllables without tripping over your tongue. Well-behaved little children soon to become decent adults who would floor the gas pedal, impatient to get to the boredom of their chalet.

It was now six months to the day since she'd made her expedition to the Laurentians, and she had always promised herself that she'd celebrate the anniversary by returning to this road one last time, to see where exactly things had started to change. Because something had happened that night, something that had nothing to do with the night deposit vault, the dynamite, or the money.

Once there was an automobile that was travelling very fast, though the road was covered with snow. An automobile driven by a young woman who strangely resembled her, yet was different. A twin. Yes, a twin, she had a twin sister she'd never known about. A twin who drove at top speed, with the radio blaring. Usually rock. One of those songs that her twin recognized from the first chords, that she could sing along with, forgetting not a single word or the slightest intonation. Switch off the radio in mid-song, though, and she wouldn't be able to go on. Not one phrase, not one word, nothing. She had to sing along with the singer to get the impression that she knew the song by heart and was perfectly bilingual. And that night the twin was singing loudly, very loudly, in an attempt not to think about her pounding heart.

The other twin, the one who'd come back here, had become allergic to songs. Mixing words and music together like that seemed to her the worst aberration. It's hard to listen to the radio when you can't stand such mixes, so she'd decided on a boycott. No more morning radio to get yourself going, as if coffee alone couldn't do it — radio that did nothing but enrage you. It had taken her two weeks of intensive silence to detoxify herself, and a few months to discover what kind of music would find favour in her ears. The task had been arduous, but Geneviève had finally located an old record dealer who knew something besides the top ten. "I want music," she had told him, "only music, no words and no mixing. One instrument at a time is quite enough." The man had suggested Bach's cello suites and the fantasies by Telemann, which she savoured in tiny doses; they were exactly what she was looking for. Since that day she'd gone back every week to consult her old record dealer, and to discover another musician who'd had the courage not to mix everything together. A good man, that record dealer, who had much better things to do than travel the highways with the gas pedal to the floor. Maybe he'd robbed a bank too, when he was young, and had recovered from it. Because it was on the way home, yes, that something had happened.

The woman who set out was intoxicated by songs, while the one who came back could no longer bear those little stories that always ended too soon. When she needed a story, she would curl up in her easy chair with a blanket over her knees and plunge into a good thick novel that she could read at her own speed, without haste, and without ever being annoyed by a word from the sponsor. At such times she felt as if she'd rediscovered a distant friend, one who was all the more precious because he never asked her for anything.

The woman who set out listened to songs not just on the radio but on television too. As if the mix of words and music wasn't enough, you got another one, in pictures — and if it had nothing to do with the singer's story, tough luck. The girl who came back watched television too, now and then, but with the sound turned off so she wouldn't have to hear the dialogue, the music, or the loud announcers. She zapped from channel to channel until she landed on one of those National Geographic reports in which a lion chases a gazelle through the tall dry grass. And then she'd think back to her childhood, when the whole family gathered around the TV set to watch the match between lion and gazelle. When the lion finally sank its teeth into the neck of its prey, her brother Louis, who had already started collecting trophies, celebrated by getting out of his chair and pumping the air the way hockey players do when they score a goal. Her mother conscientiously played her part, that of a refined and sensitive woman, by closing her eyes and feeling sorry for the poor gazelle. Her father, who saw himself as the incarnation of pure reason, never took sides, though that didn't stop him from commenting sarcastically on his wife's squeamishness: you can't expect a lion to eat tofu, that's nature....

Only Geneviève didn't react. She envied her father, her mother, and her brother, who had their roles down pat and knew exactly what they were supposed to say. Nothing seemed more natural to them than to take a stand. Geneviève had never been able to do that, and now, ten years later, she still didn't know what she was supposed to think about anything. While she had always known what she didn't want, she was barely beginning to know what she did.

Geneviève turned off the highway onto the little winding road, where she was finally allowed to drive slowly, very slowly, as all drivers did instinctively as soon as they spied the luxurious chalets on the outskirts of the village; there's no better place than a classy neighbourhood to get nailed with a speeding ticket.

She drove through the village, paying no attention to the pricey inns or the little white church, which was still deserted. There was no point worrying about the setting, which she'd barely noticed the first time. It was at the exit from the village, once she'd gone past the garage, that everything had got under way. A dog — the garage dog, most likely — had barked as she drove past. She had brought her hand to her heart, which had been pounding like thunder. If a barking dog had such an effect on her, what would it be like when she parked in front of the bank and dropped the dynamite into the vault? She'd never be able to do it. A brand-new voice that she didn't know, a voice that was calm and assured, had settled into her head and taken over. Immediately her heart had slowed down and she'd only had to follow instructions meekly: stop the engine, deposit the sticks of dynamite in the vault, walk away, unrolling the wire, take shelter.... It was a dream, a dream that even the explosion hadn't disturbed. Then she'd bent down to gather up the still-warm bags of money, and once again she had listened to the voice, which advised her to sweep away her footprints.

And now the dream was over. The bankers had replaced the vault and gone back to business as if nothing had happened. If there had ever been an explosion, it hadn't left the slightest trace — not even in the newspapers, which had devoted only a few lines to the story. An attempt that had failed miserably, if you believed the reporter, and we must always believe reporters. No witness or accomplice or confidant. No one would ever track her down; she could sleep in peace and dream about something besides the gutted vault.

Geneviève didn't bother to get out of her car or even switch off the engine. She simply looked at the front of the bank, so that this image would replace the old one and permeate her brain; then she got back on the road and headed in the opposite direction, drove once more through the village without looking at it, and turned onto the highway again, where she drove faster and faster until she was over the limit.

It was at that moment, that very moment when it was all over, that, six months earlier, her heart had started to race again. A terrible thudding had echoed as far as the body of her car, as if giant hands had grabbed hold of it and were shaking it. She had gradually managed to get it under control, bringing it down to a hundred and twenty, then a hundred, as if she were matching her heartbeats to the little red speedometer needle. And once again she had heard the voice: *Slow down, Geneviève, it would be really stupid to get stopped for speeding…. Eighty kilometres an hour, eighty beats a minute, nerves normal, everything's fine, the road is empty, the pavement's nearly dry, your mind is crystal clear, magnificently lucid, don't turn on the radio, nothing but silence….*

Slow down. Safety advice, nothing more. Indeed, it would have been really stupid to be stopped for speeding by some zealous policeman who opened the trunk just to take a look. But it would also have been really stupid not to go on following that advice. Slow down. There's no hurry.

Drive tranquilly and let the others pass you. Forget the instructions of your parents and your teachers, who keep telling you that you have to surpass yourself, which is an idiotic expression anyway; where can you go once you've surpassed yourself?

Get to know music one instrument at a time, with no mixing. Read a good novel, snugly wrapped in a blanket. Work too, because you have to, but choose an occupation that's nice and easy, one you can do without racking your brain. Repeat simple movements, movements that demand just enough concentration but allow your mind to drift. Leave it to others to collect trophies, let them have the pleasure of surpassing one another, and slow down. Eighty, seventy, sixty kilometres an hour. The road is clear, the ideas come by themselves, they don't need to be forced.

And what about sex? Don't you miss it sometimes?

Yes, a little.

Some day, maybe, on the condition that I meet someone who's not in a hurry, who has nothing to prove, who doesn't worry about performance, a man who waits till he finds his rhythm before he speaks — before he does anything, in fact.

A man who doesn't want to know everything — not like the girlfriends of her adolescence, who used to fill her room with smoke and torment her till she finally gave them a shred of a secret, which they threw themselves on like vultures. Because that seemed to be all they were interested in, Geneviève had made some up. And the more intimate they seemed, the more her friends feasted on them. One day, tired of serving up scraps of her soul, she kicked them out. She was sixteen at the time and her mother was always worried; "What's happening to your friends? You're always alone, it's not normal at your age...." Mimicking her psychological jargon, Geneviève had asked her at what age, in fact, it *was* normal to free oneself from the tyranny of relationships. Her mother's bewilderment had lasted a few days; then she had gone back on the offensive, after con-

sulting her textbooks, her professors, and her fellow thera-
pists. So she wanted to dialogue — or rather, to wrench
confidences from her? No thanks, madame, I prefer silence.
Or talking with Donald, who never asks anyone for anything.

Guillaume too was addicted to discussing relationships:
"You're always alone, it's not normal, you never go out...."
A few times, to make him happy, she'd gone with him to
see his Friday-night friends. She hadn't liked Raphaël, who
had the shifty eyes of a con man, and she had liked Francis
even less — he was always ogling her breasts and trying to
impress her by spouting witticisms he probably didn't understand himself. The only one she'd liked at all was Alex,
a secretive young man who seemed uncomfortable looking at her. The young males didn't engage in a riot of confidences the way her girlfriends did; they played pool, rented
videos, and traded jokes. That had seemed healthier to her
until she realized that every single remark they made was
a pretext for competition. No thanks. And then their obsession with collecting trophies.... That was precisely what she
couldn't stand about Guillaume any more, and it had taken
her so long to realize it. He wanted to go to the States to
study, then to England; he hoped that she'd go to school
too, that she'd collect degrees and join him in the climb up
the organizational charts. If his ambition had been moti-
vated by a spirit of revenge, or by chronic insecurity, she
could have got used to it. But Guillaume had simply chosen the easiest way: he was ambitious out of laziness.

And what about sex? Some day, maybe. It would come
along quite naturally, like everything else, when all the rest
was going the way she wanted: a quiet little job, a bank
account that was growing as she emptied her cardboard
cartons — no hurry, just one more year and the last carton
would finally be empty. All she'd have to do then was sell
her business. But why sell it, for that matter? There was no
rush, she'd have plenty of time to think about that.

When she was finally back in the city, she told herself

that, all in all, her trip had been profitable, and that she should write herself a prescription: repeat every six months and perhaps more frequently, as needed, but don't overdo it.

She was just about to shut the car door, satisfied with her day, when her heart began pounding again; on the floor she had just spotted the plastic broom, the same broom she'd used to erase her footprints, still there under the seat. One day a minuscule fragment of plastic, safely stowed in a bag, would be put under her nose: "This is exhibit number twelve, Your Honour," the prosecutor would say in his fine stentorian voice. Exhibit number twelve, yes; if she had overlooked a detail like this, she'd undoubtedly forgotten others that were far more important.

Immediately, she got back in her car to get rid of her broom, dropping it into a service-station garbage can. She tossed worried glances to left and right, as if it were a hideous crime to dispose of a broom in a garbage can. Finally she went home, where, for the first time in a long while, she mentally reviewed all her little hiding places, trying to reason with herself: it's over now, nobody will ever track me down, I'll deny everything, if there were any evidence I'd have been arrested ages ago, anyway I can afford a lawyer, they'll never find anything, that's a stupid idea; it's harder to get rid of an idea than a broom, but I'll do it, I have to.

After that she tried to relax by listening to music, but with no success, and she had to break down and take a sleeping pill. She had just enough time before falling asleep to tell herself that she wasn't really afraid of policemen, judges, or prison; let them sentence her, if it was absolutely necessary, as long as they left her the dry-cleaning shop. Donald would hold the fort while he waited for her to come back. I'll pay the fine, if you want. I'll pay till the end of my days, but leave me my dry-cleaning shop.

Chapter 16

To get started, the player first had to undress the girl by moving the cursor to an article of her clothing, where he had to click the mouse; then, under "pick up" on the menu, he had to click again. A synthetic voice would let out a scandalized little cry while numbers tumbled in a window at the lower left-hand corner. As in all self-respecting video games, the points weren't counted in mere units, or even in tens or hundreds, but in millions and billions. Any man who'd shown such audacity and skill deserved a reward, it was only fair.

Once the girl was naked, he could modify to his own liking the size of her breasts and buttocks, the length of her legs, or the colour of her hair. It was impossible, however, to enrich her vocabulary, which was limited to a dozen words. On the other hand, her palette of sighs, grunts, and cries of ecstasy was very broad.

Then the actual game could begin. Once the player had chosen his favourite orifice, he went back to the menu and pointed to the object he wanted to penetrate there. Dildo, candle, popsicle, or nail-studded stick then appeared instantaneously in the girl's hand, and she used it as you might imagine, with little cries and a rolling of eyes. The player had only to admire the show and, if he so desired, to sort things out with his mouse as best he could.

Brodeur sometimes logged onto this network late at night, when he wanted a change of pace after bringing his files up to date. It was hard to imagine that this kind of diversion was destined to have a great future. The images, pirated from some run-of-the-mill magazine, were mediocre, especially when you used the "close-up" function; the soundtrack definitely left something to be desired, and the animation was downright laughable: once the girl started rolling her eyes, there was no stopping her.

In another few years people who enjoyed this kind of sensation, decked out in gloves, headsets, and judiciously arranged sensors, would be able to treat themselves to sublime nights with the movie stars of their choice, in virtual reality. Brodeur's colleagues, with whom he'd discussed the prospect, seemed to see only advantages: since these programs could be created by the first computer scientist who came along, and since the images would be synthetic, organized crime would lose its hold on the sex industry. Pimps would be reduced to unemployment, as would prostitutes, which would cut down crowding in both the courts and the hospitals, and the very frontiers of democracy would be pushed back: the most powerful monarchs, the wealthiest capitalists, and the most fawned-over stars have never dreamed of so vast a harem, soon to be accessible to any Tom, Dick, or Harry. And while they waited for this age of clean, democratic, victimless pornography to arrive, it was enough to calm down the puritans and the feminists if they set off the decline by carrying out a few raids on massage parlours and directing the migration of hookers from one street corner to another.

Brodeur wasn't sure what to think of his colleagues' futuristic ravings, but he was very disappointed that he hadn't found what he was looking for. A list of girls who had put on erotic shows or worked in massage parlours didn't exist, and most likely it never would; it would be endless, it would take huge resources to keep it up to date, and most of those girls had never done any harm, so why keep a file on them anyway?

Was there a list of their employers, at least, or something he could fall back on? That could always be found, they told him, before handing over, with a little smile, a list of prostitutes the police had a file on (the dumbest first-year student in police techniques could have done a better job), a copy of the Yellow Pages, and an access code that would let him log onto a pornographic site free of charge: forget it, Brodeur, and have some fun.

All the same, he'd copied the list of prostitutes into his own computer, without giving it much credence. If the girl he was looking for was sharp enough to be involved in such a neat little bank heist, she certainly wasn't the type to work the street, let alone get arrested.

After that he used the free time left from his other investigations to check out everything the city and surroundings had to offer by way of establishments that offered their customers erotic shows. When he had the time, he would sit at a table and watch the girls while he sucked on a Coke. It seemed to him an excellent method for forgetting Suzanne, and his therapy worked so well that he wouldn't have recognized her if they'd met on the street. Suzanne, you say? We've met before? No, I'm afraid I don't remember....

The only problem was that his therapy had perhaps worked too well: all the images were actually superimposed, and the girl of his dreams, who was dancing like a robot to an electronic rhythm, was no more exciting than the synthetic one who rolled her eyes on his computer screen. Maybe his colleagues were right when they said this was the inevitable future of pornography: in men's minds there would be only one image, hazier and hazier, which would finally disappear. And then they would contemplate, as Brodeur had so often done, running an ad in the Companions Wanted section: *Young man with desire out of control seeks young woman with all her clothes on.*

When he got to this point in his thoughts, Brodeur

quickly finished his Coke and, suddenly remembering the pretext that had brought him here, asked to meet the boss. Like the dancers they hired, these men were generally interchangeable. Always dressed with suspect elegance — some even wore tuxedos — they invariably welcomed him by letting him know, in an unctuous tone, that they had good friends in the police, that they would be honoured to number him among their clientele, and that they would of course offer him, along with a free drink, their full and complete cooperation.

Then Brodeur would shut himself away in the office to consult their registers, which were needless to say so meticulously kept up that they too were suspect. As most were computerized, he had access to a list of all the dancers who had ever worked in the establishment. Given the high turnover rate, the list was often long, but he was able to do an initial screening on the spot by eliminating black and Asian women, and then those who were still working a long time after December the 19th; if the girl had come into even part of the take, there was a strong possibility that she'd given up the profession or, at the very least, treated herself to a long vacation.

That was generally when he'd be visited by a waitress, who would shut the door behind her, then place a drink on his desk and brush against him, apparently inadvertently: can I help you? Anything at all....

He'd ask her about certain girls who were no longer on the list, but he'd get only evasive replies. While the bosses, anxious to avoid problems, were always keen to cooperate, the girls were invariably reluctant. If he'd learned nothing from Nathalie, whom he knew very well, he wouldn't get anything more from these strangers. Brodeur didn't push it; you had to respect their solidarity.

Then he went home to copy the list into his own computer, and got started on a painstaking task that would keep him busy till morning. First he had to locate the Manons, Johannes, and Julies who were hiding out as Roxanes,

Christelles, and Priscillas. To do this he used lists he'd copied out in the offices of dancers' placement agencies, much longer but also more precise: the cheques have to end up somewhere. Even so, this information was unconfirmed: the same Julie could dance under a variety of names, while several girls might share the same name. He also had to reckon with numerous changes of address, and the endless chains of false names that allow some girls to keep getting unemployment insurance while they work.

Next, he eliminated from his list girls who'd been transferred to Lebel-sur-Quévillon, Chicoutimi, or Fredericton during the month of December, and placed in another, lower priority file those who had never stopped working. Then he logged onto the system and checked to see if the remaining girls had a driver's licence, and if they'd ever been involved with bank robbers or dynamite. Finally, he studied their credit files and rejected those who had taken out loans over the past few months; conversely, he paid particular attention to those who had paid off a loan prematurely.

When there was no one left on his list, all he had to do to rest his eyes was make a synthetic girl appear.

"Hi! My name is Nancy."

"Hi!" he replied automatically, then quickly tore off her clothes. He'd have preferred to leave them on, even to put her in a winter coat, but then he couldn't have gone on to the next levels. He never hesitated, though, to cut the sound; the repeated *wannafuck*s were intolerable, and it was hard to imagine a girl who would utter cries of ecstasy while she was buying dynamite.

He used his mouse to give her breasts more volume, lengthen her legs, and top her off with a red wig. All she needed was dark glasses and she'd match the Identikit picture. Brodeur had often resisted the urge to take a felt pen and draw them directly on the screen. They would of course stay suspended in the air whenever she crouched down, but that wouldn't be much more ridiculous than watching her eyes spin like tops.

Once upon a time there was a young redhead who bought two sticks of dynamite — let's say this candle, for want of anything better. She squats, yes, like that, and hides it as best she can while waiting to give it to her boyfriend. And so the candle disappears, along with the redhead. Game over.

But why would the boyfriend send the girl to buy the dynamite instead of doing it himself? And what if we suppose that Nancy didn't have a boyfriend? That she herself placed the sticks of dynamite in the night deposit vault?

The girl takes cover, goes back to the vault, crouches to pick up the two hundred and fifty thousand points accumulating at the bottom of the screen, then stands up and looks at her footprints in the snow: dainty little footprints, left by a woman's boots.... She crouches again to sweep them away, then gets in her car, tosses her broom out the window, and goes home with nobody the wiser.

And after that? What happens after that, Nancy? Game over? Life's not a video game — nothing is ever finished, that would be too easy.

Now the girl is all alone in her car and her heart is pounding. A girl on her own who has committed the perfect robbery, with no accomplices or witnesses. And then? She has to do something with the money, and money always leaves a trail. Suppose you have two hundred and fifty thousand dollars in small bills; where would you hide it? You can't deposit it in the bank, after all.

Nancy's eyes started rolling faster and faster, as if she were trying to hypnotize herself. You're imagining things, she told him, so distinctly that he checked to see if the sound was still turned off. You're imagining things, man; maybe that stacked redhead existed only in Thériault's imagination, he'd have said anything for a cigarette. And even if she does exist, who knows what you'd find if you took off her wig, her dark glasses, and her padded bra? Did it ever occur to you, Brodeur, to made a list of all the transvestites in the province? Of course not; you aren't interested in transvestites, or in bank heists, for that matter. You think you're so smart, with your lists and your reasoning, but the truth is, Brodeur, your own perseverance is suspect. You're looking for images, nothing but images; you just want an eyeful, because you're afraid of real girls. Give up, Brodeur, turn off the computer and go to bed, it's late. Think about me before you fall asleep, maybe that'll help.

"Good night, Nancy," Brodeur murmured into the silence of his living-room.

As no one responded, and as he couldn't bear the "game over" that filled the screen, he went back to his files; you're wrong, Nancy dear, if you think you can get me down. You're the one who's afraid. You have to be really afraid to use such petty arguments. I may be on the wrong track but I'll follow it to the end. When I've finished with the dancers, I'll go to those places where the girls disguise themselves and put on private shows, starting with the fanciest ones: Le Classy, which sends a limousine to pick up clients; Dreams of New York, near the airport, satisfaction between flights guaranteed; Sensations Inc., open 24 hours, we take Visa, Mastercard, American Express; Le Pussy, where all your dreams become reality and personal cheques are accepted. I'll even check out the girls who sigh over the phone, if necessary, but I won't give up.

Brodeur kept working until the lines on his computer screen began to dance. He turned it off then, but he went on muttering as he brushed his teeth and got into his pyjamas, and he was still muttering when he lay down in bed and switched off the light. Sometimes he tried to reconstruct Nancy's face in the dark, to fling an obscenity at her, but all he saw was a blank screen.

Unable to sleep, he got up and went to the bathroom for a sleeping pill. What else is left when you can't even picture Nancy?

While waiting for the pill to work, he turned on his computer again, in case one of the bottles he'd cast into the sea had finally reached shore.

Dynamite, sand, dancer? If I were you I'd go to Le Pussy.

He rubbed his eyes and read the message, signed "Ronald," ten times. The name meant nothing to him, but it had to be a colleague, a colleague who had access to G-12, who was acquainted with the girls at Le Pussy and knew something — Le Pussy, which was exploited by policemen, and dammit, he finally had a real trail, why had he taken that sleeping pill? How could he get in touch with this Ronald, who hadn't left a number? A computer nerd could probably trace the call, but who wanted to talk to a computer nerd? Get yourself over to Le Pussy as soon as possible, track down this girl who's stacked, who has some kind of an accent, and who's no longer working at Le Pussy or anywhere else, this girl who has a driver's licence and no debts, find this girl — a real girl, Nancy, a real girl — and ask her some questions and listen to anything she says in reply, even lies, because they'll be spoken by a real voice.

CHAPTER 17

"I'd have done the same thing. Most people would come up with a restaurant or a bar, not a dry-cleaner's. It's an excellent idea, though; the customers pay cash, so every week you can deposit a little more than you've actually taken in. You just have to be patient and the deed is done. Yes, the more I think about it, the more I'm sure it's what I would have done. Mind if I smoke?"

"Go ahead."

Brodeur didn't look at all like the man Geneviève had been expecting for so long. He wasn't in uniform — not even a trench coat, which would have been ridiculous in this heat wave; instead he was wearing sneakers, beige slacks with an imperfect crease (what else can you expect from permanent press?), and a shirt that, in the front, at least, looked properly ironed. As he'd just got out of his car, though, it was safe to assume that the back was wrinkled.

It was precisely at that moment, when he was getting out of his car, that she had recognized him; some day a man would come along, one who wasn't a regular customer and wasn't bringing clothes to be cleaned. He would linger at the window for a moment, look again at the scrap of paper where he'd noted the address, and finally walk in and reel off exactly this kind of remark. Not an accusation, no, just one of those remarks tossed into the air the way cops do in the movies. For such a tactic to work, though, the cop has to observe the suspect's reaction. Why was this one finding it so hard to meet her eyes?

"Allow me to introduce myself. Detective Lieutenant Brodeur, Sûreté du Québec."

"How do you do?"

He was a lot younger and a lot more nervous than she'd imagined. His hand shook when he pulled the cigarette from the package, and he nearly burned himself when he struck the match. Judging by his yellow fingers and the butt he'd mashed into the sidewalk just before coming inside, he must be an inveterate smoker who'd struck several thousand matches in his lifetime. Maybe he simply hadn't slept well; the bags under his eyes were big enough to make shaving difficult. Or maybe he was the kind of man who develops ulcers, as her mother would have decreed — the kind for whom there were no viruses or germs, only emotions.

"Nice music," he said finally, after taking his first drag. "What is it?"

"Bach's Partita for Violin. I'm glad you like it. I find it restful."

"More restful than the kind you hear at Le Pussy."

"Don't worry, Lieutenant Brodeur, I've seen hundreds of customers and I have no memory for faces. Whatever goes on at Le Pussy stays at Le Pussy. Have we met before?"

"No, certainly not. I'd have remembered. And I'm not in the habit of.... Are you alone?"

"For the time being, yes," she replied, after a long silence, still looking him squarely in the eyes. "But I don't perform any more, if that's what you want."

"No, it's not that."

The good old tactics she'd used so often at Le Pussy, when a customer tried going too far, worked wonderfully well: above all, don't get angry; just give him a weary look, without turning off the commercial smile, and a man will feel like a schoolboy caught in the act. (It's not about muscles, as Bob would have said; it's not about karate, it's in the eyes that it happens.) The dry-cleaner's customers, many of whom had tried to seduce her, had received the same treatment, with the same results. When weariness and a commercial smile run aground, silence works miracles. You just have to let them talk, without ever losing your little smile, and they'll reel off their compliments, jokes, or tales of their exploits, faster and faster, and they'll always come to realize on their own just how ridiculous they are.

The tactic worked equally well with policemen, so it seemed. Geneviève stood there, perfectly still, doing her best to copy the *Mona Lisa*'s smile, while Brodeur sucked on his cigarette as he nervously scanned the back of the shop. He had asked a question, she had answered it. If he wanted to know more about Donald, he had only to ask. It would be her pleasure to tell him that her employee was busy arranging his friend's funeral, and that she'd given him the rest of the week off. If he was at all insistent she could also rhyme off his age, weight, height, and social insurance number, but something told her he already had this information. He hadn't just dropped in here by chance; he must have prepared himself....

"How long ago did you buy this business?"

"Six months," replied Geneviève, after pretending to think it over for a while. (It's not as easy as it seems to remember all the months of the year, in order: February, March, April, and so on up to July. Don't talk too fast, don't try to justify yourself, you'll look guilty; you have to attack this man with silence, that's his weak point.)

There was something downright weird about the situation; wasn't it the suspect who was supposed to burn his fingers and bite his lips? Geneviève was a little worried, of course, but mostly she was relieved that he'd finally come. If she hadn't restrained herself, she would even have congratulated him for choosing the best possible moment for his interrogation: the middle of a summer afternoon, the slack season par excellence, and while Donald was off, for he would certainly have been intrigued.

"Look, let me get to the point..."

"Would you like a candy? Help yourself...."

Disconcerted by her innocent reply, he put the cigarette he'd just extracted back in the package, started to take a candy, then had second thoughts. This time he managed to strike his match without burning his fingers — that was something, anyway.

"I smoke too much, I know, I'm going to stop..."

"You don't have to. Smokers are good customers. And if they've got cats too.... How many do you have?"

"Cats? Just one. But..."

"From the cat hair on your pants. I have an eye for those things."

"Ah yes, no matter how much I brush.... Look, there's something about your story that intrigues me, Mademoiselle Vallières. You bought this business six months ago. The trouble is, there's no trace anywhere of the transaction. There'd normally be a cheque. People don't carry seventy-five thousand dollars around in their pockets...."

Geneviève was still smiling; all the cards were finally on the table. If she managed to get out of this — and she'd prepared herself so well that she wouldn't fail — it would be over, really and truly over.

She'd have to be careful not to talk too fast, though. There was no rush. It's true, you don't carry seventy-five thousand dollars around in your pocket, but that was just stating the obvious; you still had to give the policeman time to formulate the remark as a question, as the grammar teachers put it: "Isn't that so, Mademoiselle Vallières? What do you think, Mademoiselle Vallières?"

That was certainly how he would pick up the thread when Geneviève had finished with the customer who'd just come in. *And what do you want?*

"These are my husband's slacks, there's a spot right

here.... And my dress too, you have to be very careful..."

"Okay, I'll be on my way now, Mademoiselle Vallières, I can see you're busy...."

No, don't go yet, I'll only be two minutes, and you, can't you take better care of your clothes? Do you think I enjoy cleaning spots? Don't go, officer, you just got here....

Brodeur really managed to surprise her; instead of waiting for her response, he took advantage of the old lady's arrival to leave quietly, almost on tiptoe. If this was a tactic, it was a hard one to understand.

Geneviève had a little trouble recovering her professional reflexes, but she conscientiously jotted some figures on the ticket, which she then folded in two and tore along the dotted line. It was a comforting act, and she even gave the old lady a polite smile. (*Thanks for reminding me. You're quite right: I've got nothing better to do than clean clothes.*)

§

Beginning in mid-August, if the weather looked bad, customers would start bringing in their raincoats. Then would come the suits and uniforms of people returning from their vacations, and finally the fall coats. Luckily there were little old ladies now and then to ward off boredom; otherwise she'd have been condemned to clean the counter, read novels, listen to music, or play backgammon with Donald. For a dry-cleaner, there's no worse season than summer.

Never had Geneviève so looked forward to autumn, then winter, spring, and yet another autumn, dozens more autumns, and snow, rain, blizzards, mud, and factories that spat their soot all over everything, so she could fill her time cleaning and pressing clothes, wrapping them in plastic, hanging them on the conveyor, keeping her hands busy and not thinking about anything, at least not for long.

What about sex, don't you miss it sometimes? When such questions go through your mind, you can always shrug and focus confidently on your work. But the question is still there, hanging in the air, waiting for an answer — the only answer possible. She needed time, that was all. But when you can't keep your hands busy, ideas obsess you and you're no longer sure of anything.

How did he manage to track her down? The question follows Geneviève to the back of her shop, where she takes the old lady's cleaning. From force of habit, she turns the trouser pockets inside out to shake out the grit that always accumulates there; if there's a little piece of chewing gum, it's best to get rid of it before you press the pants. She begins to extract the Kleenex fragments and grains of sand that are stuck there, one at a time, but in the end she'll toss the trousers into the machine; since she won't be able to drive the question out of her head, she may as well tackle it head on. Fill the container, close the lid, press the button, and put both hands on the machine to feel the vibrations, the way Donald does when he's upset about something. Close your eyes and imagine a courtroom, yet again.

"Ladies and gentlemen, all rise."

The section reserved for the public is empty. There is no one but Lieutenant Brodeur, who's biting his nails in the witness box, waiting for the hearing to begin.

Be patient another few moments, please, lieutenant; see, I'd always pictured you as old, some geezer with white hair and a friendly face like a St. Bernard, you know the type. I need time to sort out my mental images, as my mother would say. Lieutenant Brodeur: young, cute, very nervous, but he tries to calm down by petting his cat before he interrogates suspects. So here we are.

"Let's go back to the beginning, Lieutenant Brodeur, since we have to." (That's right, show our impatience right away.) "Did you find any fingerprints at the scene of the crime?"

"No, Your Honour. The defendant must have been wearing gloves, Your Honour."

"I think so too, Lieutenant Brodeur. There were no prints, then. Did you at least think of analysing the tracks the tires left in the snow?"

"Obviously, Your Honour, but there are millions of tires just

like those..."

"And there's a good chance the defendant has had her tires changed in the meantime, said tires having now been retreaded or recycled to make sandals. Is that correct, Lieutenant Brodeur?"

"Undoubtedly, Your Honour."

"Very well. I imagine she wasn't so foolish as to leave her wallet at the scene of the crime?"

"No indeed, Your Honour."

"Then perhaps you're going to tell me that you found a hair in the snow, that you've placed said hair in a device that allowed you to learn from its DNA that the name of the suspect was Geneviève Vallières, and that she'd just bought a dry-cleaning shop? Or that you'd marked the bills in the vault in case a thief should turn up? But with evidence like that, Lieutenant Brodeur, why wait nine months before laying charges? Am I correct, Lieutenant Brodeur, when I state that you have no material evidence?"

"Quite correct, Your Honour. Aside from exhibit number one..."

"Surely you aren't going to show me that little piece of plastic. Have you found the rest of the broom, at least?"

"No, Your Honour. You're right, Your Honour: there's no evidence."

"As you can see, I'm delighted. But if you've worked so hard to appear before us, we must conclude that you have some witnesses. We're very curious to hear from them, Lieutenant Brodeur. Since I believe the defendant acted alone, the witness cannot be an accomplice. And since she's never said a word to anyone.... Unless she talked in her sleep?"

"In fact, I'd like to call my first witness, Your Honour."

"Very well. And who is that?"

"A pillow, Your Honour. I realize there's something odd about it, but I'd like to point out that this is the suspect's personal pillow, Your Honour."

"Would you mind repeating that?"

"A pillow, Your Honour... If she did talk in her sleep...."

And again Geneviève asks Brodeur to repeat what he's just said, though she has heard him perfectly well. It's not so much his words that are troubling her as the tone of his voice. Deep and gruff and warm. This man has circles under his eyes and he smokes like a chimney, but he speaks in a calm, soothing tone, and the rest of the trial bears no resemblance to what she's imagined so often. There's no longer an old, white-haired cop leaving the courtroom sheepishly after the judge asks if he has handcuffed the pillow and read it its rights; there is Brodeur, a suddenly relaxed Brodeur who says nothing more, but holds her gaze. And then he walks out, very slowly, leaving Geneviève all alone in her deserted store, wondering if it's a good idea to let a machine shake up your body. Why did he walk out like that, why didn't he ask all his questions at the same time, to get it over with and move on to something else?

And what do you want to move on to, Geneviève? He'll be back one of these days, you know he'll be back. Why is that reassuring when it ought to have you worried? Shake me up a little more, machine.

§

Brodeur stays in the shower long after the hot water tank has emptied. Then he fixes himself a cup of decaff instant coffee, and sits down at his computer.

Geneviève Vallières. Age twenty-two. Not a hint of a police file, even for simple possession of a used hash pipe. Spotless driving record without a single speeding ticket. A circumspect young woman. Works for six months at Le Pussy, where her gymnast act is very popular; leaves her job two weeks to the day after the night deposit vault blows up. Circumspect again. But she tells her boss, who still has a tear in his eye when he thinks of it, that she's going to have a church wedding, which she hasn't had. It takes more than a lie to a boss or a broken engagement to incriminate a person, of course, even though she's made her first mistake: a young girl who leaves Le Pussy doesn't need to make up a reason.

There are no extravagant expenditures and she continues to pay off her car loan every month, which would seem to exonerate her; but why did she suddenly stop using her credit card in January?

She then makes her second mistake, a much more serious one, by purchasing her business without a mortgage and without a trace of a transfer of funds or a cheque drawn on her account.

A small operation that's doing a brisk business, to judge by the bank deposits she makes every week. Very brisk, even. At the limits of plausibility. Still, it's possible; if my dry-cleaner looked like her, I'd probably go more often...

"Hi! I'm Nancy."

"Hi!"

First, let's take off the red wig. Ordinary brown hair. And brown eyes, sometimes very bright and sometimes a little tired, always changing — eyes that shoot strange looks at you, as if she were in another place or, rather, in another time. Another time, yes: neither early nor late, but elsewhere in time. That's disturbing, Ms. Nancy. And so much better than your own eyes that spin like tops.

An attractive voice, too, with that strange accent you come down with in private school. *An accent that's not exactly French from France, but something like it.* A very attractive voice, yes, nothing like your "wannafuck wannafuck", which sounds like Donald Duck, you poor dear. And don't carry on like that, I have no desire to put the cursor on your T-shirt and hear your scandalized "Oh!". I won't remove any of your clothes, Nancy. If I could, I'd even draw black slacks on you, and a white blouse buttoned to the neck. It was that, along with everything else, that took my breath away. It was as if someone had hurled a twenty-kilo exercise ball into my stomach, full force. I didn't see it coming. It took my breath away, Nancy. And my stomach hurts. It doesn't happen in your heart, even less in your head; it's in your stomach; of course, you can't know that it starts in the stomach and then spreads everywhere else: you get cold, moist hands and tingling lips, and your heart beats not faster but harder, and it sends your blood everywhere, to the ends of your hair. You can't imagine how exciting it can be to see a girl with her clothes on. Just try conducting an question under those conditions. Yet you have to question her, set traps for her, cast lines into the water and wait for her to bite; you need confessions, not just circumstantial evidence. She could have been in the Laurentians on the night of December 19th, just as she could have been anywhere else, and I hope she was, at the same time as I hope she was anywhere else, and try and make a computer understand that. Do *you* understand that, Nancy?

Geneviève Vallières. He still has no evidence, and probably never will have any. And no witnesses. Just one informer: the boss at Le Pussy, who vaguely remembers hearing about the sand-bag technique in the waiting-room — the police talked about it for a long time, in the presence of the girls — and who answers messages posted on the electronic bulletin board, just in case.

Geneviève Vallières, prime suspect. And all it took was a white blouse buttoned to the neck and my investigation was ruined. Game over, before I could collect even one measly point. Then again, there's no hurry. If I've waited this long I can wait a while longer. This is *my* investigation. I could have closed the book. No one forced me to go this far. And you know that better than anyone, Nancy, don't you? Why shouldn't I take my time?

If you wanted to be nice, Nancy — really nice — you'd go put some clothes on.

CHAPTER 18

Geneviève's mother spent a long time tangled in endless sentences borrowed from her husband, who had picked them out of the financial papers (globalization of markets, competitiveness, entrepreneurship — that kind of thing), before admitting that she'd finally got used to the idea: her daughter was now the owner of a *business* (she pronounced the word disdainfully — good grief, a *business*, and a *dry-cleaner's*, of all things). But she'd thought carefully about Bernard's arguments; he'd pointed out that her psychologist's practice was also a *business*. He was right, of course, *in a sense....*

Then some fire trucks drove down St. Denis Street, and their sirens brought her admissions to a halt; she took advantage of the din to sip some beer. It had never occurred to her that her office was anything as vile as a business; it was easier for her to swallow her beer than to utter that bitter word.

While she waited for the firemen to force their way through the traffic, Geneviève looked at the customers around them. These people had paid a fortune for their beer and, as a result, they were doing their best to drink it slowly. As their bikes, Lycra gear, and dark glasses had cost even more, the owners had to amortize them by showing them off to the largest number of people possible, so they'd all decided — nothing was forcing them — to congregate on a little stretch of sidewalk squeezed between the street and a brick wall. They were conscientiously playing the part their getup dictated, with beaming faces and blissful smiles, despite the clamour of conversation, the din of traffic, and the speakers spitting out jazz. Geneviève was bothered by it; how long did they have to train before they could sit on these plastic chairs whose feet got stuck in the sidewalk cracks, breathing the fumes of car exhaust and swallowing the flies that drowned in their beer, and look relaxed about it? It was her mother who had insisted on an outdoor café. Her mother, who had the quirk of drinking beer only in summer and only outside.

Though she'd have given anything to be somewhere else, Geneviève had decided to drain the cup to its dregs. The trick was to let her mother talk all she wanted, so that she wouldn't guess the real reason for the invitation. Nothing made her happier than coming here to this terrace for a beer, she was saying now; it reminded her of her youth, your father never wants to go out, yadayadayada, and just think, isn't it funny that you and I are both businesswomen, *in a sense*; if anyone had told me, back in the days when I used to drive you to your piano lessons, that one day you'd be the owner of a dry-cleaning shop, but yes, I'm used to the idea now, the only thing I care about, and I've always said this, the only thing I care about is your happiness....

She uttered that old cliché again, and Geneviève indulged her with a grateful smile; there's nothing more predictable than a mother, and that's even more true if she's a psychologist.

Geneviève let her go on talking for an hour, content most of the time to give a quick answer to her questions, then throw the ball back to her, without trying to score points herself — like a Red Army officer forced to play tennis with Stalin.

When she felt that her mother had been softened up enough by the beer and the sunshine, Geneviève tried to regain control of the match by asking a few questions about the strictly commercial aspect of her practice; then she surreptitiously led her to talk about accounting. Monique, of course, had never understood a thing about it. She never took care of *those sorts of things*. Now the ground was prepared, and Geneviève made her move:

"Speaking about *those sorts of things*, as you put it, I might want to ask you for a little favour. See, I've got some tax problems..."

"Yes, I see," Monique replied, squinting as if to say that she really did see something. "Is business bad? Do you need money?"

"No, not at all. It's actually a little too good, at least as far as the tax inspectors are concerned. You know what they're like."

"Indeed I do," her mother answered knowingly, though she'd never met a tax inspector in her life. "But why not talk to your father about all this? You know me..."

"I'd rather talk to you. You know Papa, he wants me to succeed so badly, it's becoming a bit of a burden..."

"Oh yes, I understand. I understand very well." (This time she sounded convincing.) "But what can I do for you?"

"Nothing at all. Well, practically nothing.... It's just that I have to inflate my costs to reduce my profits. Actually, I have to invent a payment. It would make sense to say that you lent me some money when I bought my business, so that I have to pay back a certain amount every month. Something like a private mortgage, just between the two of us. One that even Papa wouldn't know about..."

"Look, Geneviève, I'd be glad to help, but you have to know I'm a very bad liar...."

"Of course," replied Geneviève, though she thought her mother could have qualified her declaration. "That's exactly why I'm bringing it up with you, actually. All I want from you is permission to say, if I really have to, that you lent me some money and I'm paying you back a certain amount every month. I wouldn't like to involve you without your knowing, especially since it's fairly complicated..."

"That's all right, I trust you. How much did I lend you, exactly?"

"I don't know — how about thirty thousand? You could have sold some bonds or something like that, and given me the money in cash so it would be just between us. And I'd be paying you three hundred a month, cash. Papa wouldn't know anything about it. It would be just between us. Three hundred dollars a month, that's all."

"And you swear I won't have to lie to anybody?"

"No. Look — let's drop it, it's too complicated. I'll figure out something else.... I don't really know why I brought it up with you. But you know what they're like in the tax department. To them, you're always guilty, even if you have nothing to feel guilty about. They've got all kinds of tricks and they like to use them, especially on women.... While the real tax cheats.... No, really, let's drop it. I'm worrying over nothing. Anyway, why talk about money on such a beautiful day.... What were you saying just now, about your client?"

Only too happy to change the subject, her mother went back to the account she'd started a little earlier, of a good family man who consumed porn magazines the way others do alcohol: he claimed he absolutely had to have them, though he squandered a fortune on them and was gnawed by guilt.

"They've got eyes," Geneviève observed, without really thinking about it.

"What do you mean, eyes? I'm talking about pornography. Don't you think it's degrading?"

"When I said they've got eyes, I meant the girls. Eyes that look at him. Why not suggest that he go on buying his magazines but cut out the faces? Or even better, just the eyes. He'll get tired of them."

"You know, that's not a bad idea."

§

The afternoon stretched out peaceably on the terrace, and the customers around the two women had been replaced by others. Excited at having finally found a place to sit, these people talked very quickly at first, then slowed considerably. Maybe they had nothing more to say, or maybe they felt vaguely that if they just changed their rhythm, all of them together, time itself would stop and winter would never come.

Geneviève too felt somewhat relaxed. The beer and the sun had something to do with it, as did her satisfaction with a job well done; she'd come to the end of her mission. If Brodeur asked her where her money had come from, she'd have an answer. All she had to do now was really listen to what her mother was saying, with no hidden agenda. To her amazement, she found it interesting. Monique was talking about her male clients, onto whom Geneviève could easily graft one or another of the faces she'd seen at Le Pussy, and about her numerous female clients, whose sex lives apparently weren't totally blissful. For instance, the woman who for twenty years of marriage had always faked orgasm, and would probably go on doing so till the end of her days, convinced that sooner or later she would overcome her lesbian fantasies; and another woman who had worked as a topless waitress to pay her tuition and confessed that she'd rather enjoyed it....

Geneviève found it rather strange that both mother and daughter, each in her own way, had cashed in on the sexual woes of their contemporaries, and even stranger that, after telling her a whole pile of stories to confuse the issue, her mother talked so much about this girl who'd worked as a topless waitress because it was the only way she could save a little money and come to Montreal to go to school, who had dyed her hair to make herself believe she was somebody else, "and if you think of it, it's nothing to be ashamed of, she was doing it to pay for her education or build up some capital, what matters is getting out at the right time; topless waitresses have long been a thing of the past, of course, but the principle's the same: they can look but they can't touch. Men like that kind of image, just as women like Harlequin romances. What's important is to get out, and it doesn't much matter how. It wouldn't bother me if I found out that someone I knew was doing that kind of work — as long as it was temporary, of course. What do you think?"

"Why ask me?"

"I don't know. A feeling, I guess. Your father has the same kind of feelings, but they hit him harder than they do me. I can always try to pry these ideas out of his head, but I need more information. Is it over now?"

"If there had ever been something like that, it would be over, yes."

"That's what I thought. Good Lord, did you see the time? Bernard must be wondering what I'm doing...."

That it was her mother who found a pretext for ending the conversation stunned Geneviève. Monique got up, prattling something or other — wonderfully superficial, as she always was — and Geneviève walked slowly towards her car, trying to digest everything she'd just heard. Her mother, who'd been born in Chicoutimi, who'd come to Montreal to go to school, who had always taken obsessive care of her hair, who only drank beer outside — her mother, who had managed to tell her everything without telling her anything — as she always did.

Even in slow motion, life is much too complicated. You mustn't misuse conversations, they're even more treacherous than a beer in the sunshine, and they leave a funny aftertaste, not really bitter, but.... If anyone had told her that her mother would become her accomplice, the only one to whom it was possible to say nothing, the only one who wouldn't want to know more and would never bring the matter up again....

§

Geneviève got to her car, and walked around it to check that no one had slipped inside while she was gone. Brodeur, for instance.

There was a strange idea that had been bothering her for a while now: what if he'd been there all the time, hidden behind the seat, from the day she'd bought the dynamite? What if he'd been following her from the very beginning? What if he'd settled into her head, what if it was his voice she'd heard?

Really, that was an idiotic idea, she told herself as she finally opened her door. As far as she knew, astral travel, out-of-body experiences, and telepathy were not yet part of police procedure. That left just one possibility: a message had appeared somewhere, on the screen of some Big Brother's computer. It had taken only one questionable transaction to make a whole series of warning lights blink on, and within a fraction of a second every bank account in the country and every file in the Department of Revenue had been examined.

She'd made a mistake when she had paid cash for her business, and that had set off the system. Brodeur had just had to press a button to learn that she had once worked at Le Pussy, that she changed the oil and rotated the tires of her Honda regularly, that she'd subscribed to the Columbia Record Club for six months, and that when she was sixteen she'd asked the doctor to prescribe her first birth control pills. And then Brodeur had made the connection, God knows how, with the night deposit vault.

To calm him down she had only to douse the warning light, and then everything else would disappear like a thread into a vacuum cleaner. I paid cash, yes. I didn't know it was an offence. I'd saved some money and my mother advanced me the rest. Under the table. My father wouldn't have gone along with it, you know how it is....

It held up. Only Réjean could have contradicted the

story, and it had been some time now since a heavy purple curtain had closed on his coffin, which had then glided into the crematorium.

Maybe it could work. But there was a better way: arrange things so he didn't even ask. To do that, she'd have to attack on the only ground that Big Brother could never control, and the timing was right: in fact, she had a powerful urge to go for a stroll on that very ground.

CHAPTER 19

Whenever she gave a man her phone number, Geneviève had to wait for three days before he made up his mind to use it. Men didn't want to seem too eager, but they didn't want to risk losing out by feigning indifference either; three days was how long it took a man to protect his independence.

At the first ring Geneviève gestured to Donald, who hadn't yet had time to react, that she would answer. It had to be Brodeur; it had been noon when he first walked inside her store, and now it was twenty to twelve three days later. He had respected the delay nearly to the minute. As well as being a cop, he was a normal man.

She wasn't going to reproach him for his haste, which she was inclined to take as a compliment, but neither was she going to betray herself by answering too quickly. With her hand on the receiver, she waited for two more rings before picking it up. Girls are entitled to their little obsessions too, to show that they don't sit around waiting for the phone to ring. Then she had to pick it up, speak in a neutral tone, and feign surprise. It would be up to him to speak first, thank God, so she'd have time to get her wits back.

Brodeur — it was him, it had to be him — started by babbling some apology for his hasty departure (an urgent meeting that he'd suddenly remembered had forced him to leave in a hurry); then, in a voice that gradually took on more self-confidence, he asked her if it would be possible to continue the conversation that had been so abruptly broken off.

Geneviève replied that unfortunately she was very busy all week, but that perhaps he could come to the store on Saturday morning, if that was convenient. Immediately she could have kicked herself; she'd spoken too quickly, it sounded prepared.

Brodeur suggested coming around eleven, which she agreed to: eleven on the dot, yes, and no later; with summer hours, you see, I close at noon.

This last detail discomfited Brodeur, who wasn't sure how to interpret it, as much as it did Geneviève, who wondered if she hadn't moved a little too fast. They were silent for a moment before they both confirmed an appointment for Saturday at eleven on the dot, and they waited a little longer than necessary before hanging up, neither of them wanting to be the one to end the conversation.

§

Some people do their mourning on the very day of the death; it's a difficult period, but the pain evaporates along with the tears. Donald belonged to the second category of mourners, those who calmly take care of the formalities and get on with their lives as if nothing has happened. They keep the situation under control for a few months, a few years even, until their grief hits them like a sledgehammer when they least expect it; then they sink into a deep depression and don't know what's causing it. Since Réjean's death, Donald had felt light, even cheerful, and it was only out of concern for the proprieties that he assumed a gloomy expression. Maybe someday he'd pay the price for his indifference, he often thought, but then again, maybe he would be exempt, having done his mourning in advance.

Who could say? For the time being, he was in a wonderful mood, and he was having fun observing Geneviève: her new nervous habit of chewing her lower lip, her flushed cheeks, the way she stared into space and jumped whenever the phone rang...he wasn't going to miss clues like that. Sometimes, for the pleasure of needling her, he'd ask some trivial question while she was daydreaming; judging by how long it took her to answer, you knew she was coming back from a long journey, and was still suffering jet lag.

Donald amused himself that way for three days, until he saw her race to the phone, let it ring three times before she answered, and finally hang up as if the phone were made of crystal. When she then offered him the next Saturday off, he could have pretended to refuse, for the fun of teasing her, but he didn't have the heart. It may sound silly, but he felt almost jealous.

§

It was seven minutes to eleven when Brodeur parked his car a few streets away from the dry-cleaner's. He'd have just enough time to stretch his legs and smoke a cigarette, which would burn his throat, while repeating to himself that Geneviève was first and foremost a suspect; then he'd chew a mint to freshen his breath, something he never did before an interrogation, and it was all so complicated that it was best not to think about it; just put one foot in front of the other, open the door, and after that, he'd see.

Geneviève had done her best not to look at the clock all morning, but when she heard the tinkling bells she knew it was exactly two minutes to eleven. As she was attempting to look busy, before emerging from the back of the shop she took a moment to run a lint brush over her clothes again, and to check herself in the mirror. She moved a lock of hair so it wouldn't appear freshly combed, and bit her lips, which needed some colour.

On the stroke of eleven, she finally appeared behind

the counter. Brodeur barely looked at her. Trying to seem casual, most likely, he bent his head as if to hear the music better.

"What's that playing?" he finally managed to get out, after clearing his throat.

Geneviève — who of course knew the answer, since she'd chosen the disc with great care — took the time to listen to a few bars, pretending to think. Unless he was truly stupid, Brodeur would not make the mistake of tackling her head-on. He would advance slowly, on tiptoe, and cast his lines into the water. She could afford to play along for a few moments; there was no rush. Men like feeling they're in control of a situation.

"*Syrinx*," she said finally.

After a brief hesitation, she added that it was by Debussy. (You must never give people one-word answers; they sound rude. And since you should avoid the opposite extreme too, she restrained herself from adding that it was a solo for flute, something he could no doubt figure out for himself.)

"Is it the music that makes you like this?"

"What do you mean?"

"You seem so calm, so relaxed, as if nothing could affect you."

"It's partly the music, partly other things. I've been working at it for quite a while."

"I can see that. But there must have been times in your life when you were more nervous."

As she'd anticipated, Brodeur would simply make vague allusions and wait for her to give herself away. How could he imagine that she'd fall into such a crude trap? Did he assume she'd leap at the first chance to account for how she'd spent the night of December 19th? He must know that nothing sounds more guilty than an alibi.

"Did you know I'm a Virgo?"

"You're a *what*?" He'd heard "virgin."

"I said I'm a Virgo. My astrological sign. But I suppose

you already know that."

"How would I know?"

"Because you saw it on your computer screen, like everything else. 'Geneviève Vallières. Age twenty-two. Virgo. Unattached. No demerit points. Uses credit card rarely. Dentition healthy. Changes oil in Honda regularly. Worked six months at Le Pussy to put together the money to buy a dry-cleaner's.... That's a good idea, you know, using the police computer. It costs less than signing up with a dating service. But is it legal?"

"What makes you think...?"

The hardest thing to do was look him directly in the eyes and still hold onto her smile. She could afford to let him stammer a little, but she mustn't give him time to land on his feet.

"You come in here but you don't bring any cleaning, you ask me the weirdest questions, then you phone to make an appointment.... For a while I thought you were on an investigation. But if you were accusing me of something, you'd have said so by now, right? So there's just one other possibility. It may not be the most elegant approach, but it's certainly original. So original that I've decided to give you a reward. On one condition, though. Do you know about Japanese marriage bureaus? You send in your photo, they match you up with a man your age, and you're allowed three meetings, that's all. And then you decide if the two of you want to get married."

"It's a bit hasty, isn't it?"

"You could say so. On the other hand, you could say you're not making any commitment. If the party they suggest doesn't suit you, you're free to start again with someone else. But still just three meetings. After that, you get married and you have the rest of your lives to get to know one another. The more I think about it, Lieutenant Brodeur, the more I tell myself it's not such a bad idea. And it's very romantic: marriage becomes the beginning of the story, not the end."

"Would you do a thing like that?"

"Absolutely. And I know what I'd suggest for the first meeting: a drive to the Laurentians. Leave in an hour. Back tonight. How does that sound?"

"Zen."

"I beg your pardon?"

"Zen. Marriage Japanese-style — the flute, the smile — very Asian. So I said 'Zen' because the word went through my mind. There's no reason you should have a monopoly on disconcerting remarks. I don't mind tossing one out myself. Comes in handy in my line of work. Now, let me warn you: I said 'Zen' but I could just as well have said 'snow tires' or 'sandbags.'"

"I prefer 'Zen.' To me, 'snow tires' sounds perverse. Shall we go?"

"I thought we were already on our way."

§

"You got me there, Lieutenant Brodeur, but I'm driving now and I'm looking at the road straight ahead of me. So you have to take charge of the bulk of the conversation now, it's only fair. And you know more about me than I do about you, right? So go ahead, impress me. That's what men usually try to do, and I'm sure you're no exception."

"Yes, I have to take charge of the conversation, but what can I talk about? Childhood memories, my parents, my education? It's so banal I'd bore myself. My favourite movies and restaurants, like in dating services? And why not my astrological sign, while we're at it? Of course, I could talk about work, but I don't want her to think it's the centre of my life, though nowadays that's fairly close to the truth...

"I..."

"Yes?"

"Nothing.... I thought you were going to say something."

"Me?" *(Of course, me. Who else? The art of achieving an*

idiotic answer in just one word.)

The situation was truly strange — they both thought so, whenever one of them opened his mouth to start a conversation that never took off. Shouldn't a normal young man and young woman on their first outing have lots to say to one another, shouldn't they get drunk on remarks rich in innuendo, toss out words that make sparks, relate so many memories that eventually they discover a coincidence they're prompted to hail as a miracle? If you think about it, maybe that's the secret of the Japanese method. As soon as the lady from the dating service has introduced the candidates, she reads them the regulation warning: watch out, beginning now anything you say can be used against you, for the rest of your lives. So all the young couple can do is exchange timid smiles, under the amused and benevolent eyes of the slightly deaf old auntie who's been designated to play chaperone.

Either that or drive slowly down the highway without saying a word, like an old couple.

§

They managed to say nothing until they passed a shopping centre on the way out of an affluent-looking village. Geneviève, who would normally have accelerated, slowed down and asked Brodeur if he needed any cash.

"No, not really. Why?"

"There's a bank there, I think."

"I know, but I don't have my card on me. Have you got one?"

"Yes, but I hardly ever use it. As you should know."

Geneviève didn't even look in Brodeur's direction to see his reaction. Instead, she rolled down her window in a fit of pique and let the wind whip her face; why did she feel obliged to provoke him? And why had she spoken when he tolerated silence so well?

Brodeur rolled down his window too, to let out the

smoke from his cigarette, and the sound of the wind rushing into the car gave him an excellent pretext for not replying. If he lived with this girl for a hundred thousand years, he'd probably never understand her. Maybe it would be best to give up on it right away.

§

They parked near a path that would take them to a remote lake surrounded by mountains so steep that it was impossible to build chalets there. Geneviève had known about it all her life, as she'd often spent her vacations here when she was a little girl. The only problem was that getting to the lake required an hour-long walk. That didn't seem to bother Geneviève, who started the climb at a rapid pace. Brodeur followed a little more slowly; what could she possibly have in mind?

"Turn around," she told him when they finally reached the lake. "Turn around and don't look."

Brodeur obeyed, though not without a strange thought going through his head: he had followed her along the path for an hour, often very close behind, but it never occurred to him to check whether she was hiding a weapon in her slacks. With his eyes closed, he tried to make the images reappear: no, she didn't have a weapon — not that kind, anyway.

Still, he was startled when he heard sounds behind him. Nothing at all like a shot, though: branches cracking, the surface of the lake breaking, then closing immediately.

"All right, you can turn around now!"

She was there, a few metres from shore, almost completely immersed. He could see nothing but her head, her shoulders, and the straps of her bathing-suit.

"There's one problem," he shouted.

"Don't tell me you're afraid of the water!"

"No, it's not that..."

"You can't swim? Don't worry, it's not very deep."

"No, it's not that either.... It's just that I don't have a bathing-suit. You should have told me."

"I totally forgot, that was silly. But it doesn't matter. I've seen men get undressed before, you know..."

"I'm sure you have," grumbled Brodeur as he slowly pulled off his shoes and socks. He hesitated briefly before unbuttoning his shirt; she would see his tanned arms and his white belly, a belly that wasn't altogether flat, either; why had he stopped working out...? Finally he pulled off his shirt, but he still hesitated to unbuckle his belt.

"I hope you don't mind if I watch."

"To tell you the truth, I do mind, a little."

"I see."

But she stayed there watching him, with a big grin that had nothing Zen about it. Maybe if he threw a rock at her? No, he had something better.

"Have I told you I'm a Pisces?"

"You're pretty fishy, I know.... Oh do you mean your astrological sign?"

That was a low blow, thought Brodeur as he finally pulled off his pants and jumped in. I tried to warn her, but never mind; she'll find out soon enough that I was captain of my water-polo team, and there was nobody as good as me at giving my opponents a mouthful.

§

They didn't sip wine or gulp oysters or nibble smoked salmon. A cheeseburger, limp fries and a can of Pepsi did the trick, and anyway that was all they could order from the former schoolbus that had been converted into a greasy spoon.

They wolfed down their banquet, then stayed for a long time at their picnic table in the shadow of a pine tree. They talked about work, about novels, movies, music, and many other things, without ever wondering if what they were saying made sense or was funny or was even worth mentioning.

They got back on the road at sunset. As they had gorged on words and were tired after the day they'd spent, they didn't say a word on the drive home. Neither of them suffered from the silence. Brodeur watched night fall around the little car and wondered if there had been a shred of truth in that story about dating Japanese-style — and, if there had been, whether it had any significance. Geneviève just drove, even more slowly than usual. And it never even occurred to her to turn on the radio.

CHAPTER 20

Some relationships come to an end in the most idiotic way imaginable: people suddenly realize that they're no longer any fun.

Francis administered the *coup de grâce* to the little gang's activities on the day he realized that they were all moving on, each in his own direction, to pursue their studies at different universities. They would come back with an MA, a Ph.D, a job, maybe even a wife. Wasn't it fitting to have a dazzling celebration of what would no doubt be their last summer of freedom?

His program for the festivities allowed for the usual activities — coke, pool, and checking out the bars — as well as, and this was the tricky part, a sexual Olympics. He envisaged a specific number of compulsory figures (seduce a certain number of real redheads, for instance, and provide evidence), with the whole thing crowned by a grand championship in which the conquests in all categories would be compiled. It was all a joke, of course, but he set out such a wealth of detail concerning the evidence they had to bring back that they didn't know if he was serious or not. A lot of white powder was consumed that night.

Raphaël was the first to give the project any credibility, lending it his enthusiastic support. He probably thought he had a good chance of winning, thanks to his sole advantage over his competitors: his father's wallet was always wide open to him.

Fortified by this support, Francis ordered Guillaume to take a position. And that was when things started to go wrong.

Guillaume, who wouldn't have needed any fallbacks to do well in such a competition, opposed it with all his might, invoking, to their great surprise, a long list of noble principles. The real reason for his refusal became clearer when he mentioned Stéphanie, a girl he'd just met and wouldn't shut up about.

Stéphanie, said Francis ironically, was the kind of girl it's always nice to have a few words with in the school corridors, especially when you need cigarettes or lecture notes. The kind of girl who seems destined to be an excellent second choice, who has always known this, and is perfectly happy about it. If you're so unwise as to tell her, after bumming a cigarette, that you expect to go to Harvard for your master's degree, she'll let you know right away, as naturally as anything, that she's going there too and — what a piece of luck — she even has a cool apartment, not expensive and just off campus, and a car to get there. That's all it takes to make you look at her very differently.

Guillaume didn't like Francis talking about Stéphanie this way, not at all, any more than Francis accepted the grand principles on which Guillaume based his refusal to take part in the Olympiad. And so the first and last activity of their final summer as unattached men, which had promised to be a permanent orgy, became a shouting match that nearly degenerated into a brawl: Guillaume and Francis grabbed one another by the collar and tried out a few dance steps. They weren't going to fist-fight; a person has enough knucklebones, big and small, no need to break your fingers into smaller pieces. But how do you extricate yourself from this situation once you're into it? They remained locked together till Raphaël and Alex finally came to separate them, to save them from making fools of themselves.

Guillaume walked out, slamming the door, delighted at the way it had ended. He'd had enough of this little gang who insisted on remaining adolescent; now he could finally devote himself to Stéphanie, on whose account he'd nearly gone into battle. Didn't that mean he truly loved her?

§

Alex was relieved that Guillaume had created this well-timed diversion, which had saved him from having to take a position on the issue at hand. If he'd been asked, he would have felt obliged to agree to take part in the Olympiad, if only to allay suspicion. He might even have tried to win, despite himself, which would only have postponed the day of reckoning.

He too had been hoping for this split, though he'd never been able to admit it. He had been clinging to his group of friends — his lifeline — for too long, which kept him from taking his fantasies by the horns, so to speak. Now he had no choice. By the end of the summer — and this was a firm commitment — he was finally going to choose his sexual orientation, once and for all. Because such a decision can't be taken lightly, he intended to use his holidays to explore all the avenues, systematically.

On the day after the shouting match, Alex went to a downtown newsstand and bought a vast assortment of pornographic magazines of every inclination. Shut up in his room, he first smoked a well-made little joint, then selected a magazine at random. He leafed through it abstractedly, trying to think as little as possible, until, without his realizing it, his index finger stopped turning the pages.

Naked women, no matter how seductive, never had this effect on him. On the contrary, his index finger tended to move even faster when the images were too explicit. But if they showed a couple caught in action, his finger was more likely to pause in mid-air for a moment — and the saliva on it would actually have time to dry if the couple consisted of two men.

From the index-finger test he moved on to vision persistence. Now that his tastes had been refined, he went to a video club that had an automatic dispenser and rented a number of films whose stars were exclusively male. He sometimes watched three in a row before he lay down on his bed in the dark and let hundreds of the scenes he'd saved be erased, until only the most exciting ones were left. And to his great surprise, they never featured the stars of those films; despite their amazing screen presence, those muscular young men never passed the persistence test. Instead, the scenes that held his attention dwelt on some of the minor characters on whom the camera lingered all too rarely.

Carrying on with his explorations, he finally worked up the courage to venture into a certain bar in the gay village, where he soon became a fan of a kind of show that men of a certain age and American tourists are partial to. The dancers follow one another on a little illuminated stage, the ritual nearly identical to that of the girls who ply the same trade: the first dance gives viewers an appetite by offering them sailor, cowboy, or biker costumes to admire (for the tourists there were also a lumberjack and a Mountie), the second shows them how these costumes can be peeled off as slowly as possible, while the third finally reveals what the costumes have been hiding. Because the dancers doubled as waiters and their work clothes usually consisted of a G-string, it was rare for the audience to make any dramatic discoveries.

Alex never sat by the stage. Athletes and bodybuilders, especially if they were of a significant size, didn't interest him all that much. Nor did he appreciate their tiresome habit of calling out to viewers and sending them propositions.

Since their verbal violence seemed directly proportional to their muscle mass, Alex had decided to go for a man who was neither young nor muscular. If there was any man in this room who resembled what he was looking for, he'd be found among the spectators, not on the stage.

§

Donald had only to take a seat at his usual table at The Iron Hand for the waiters to come rushing over, vying with one another to lavish attention on him, followed shortly after by an army of suitors who'd have sold their souls for the mere privilege of being seen in his company.

Donald didn't possess the charm of a movie star, let alone the power of a king. Worse yet, he didn't have two cents to rub together. All his savings had gone into Réjean's funeral — a total waste, as it turned out. Réjean had left him nothing, instead naming in his will a raging queen whom Donald didn't know from Adam, and who'd dropped out of circulation as soon as he'd got his hands on the loot.

Donald was exactly what he'd always been: a man who was rather ugly and very short, yet not a dwarf (for some that's a turn-on); a dry-cleaner by trade and, let's not mince words, very modestly hung. Those who courted him would find that out one day or another, but Donald preferred to let them wait. In the meantime, he'd have been foolish not to take advantage of the misunderstanding. Because it was a misunderstanding; there was no other explanation.

What exactly had changed since Réjean's death? All right, so his own health was excellent. Given Réjean's life-style, one could assume that Donald was immunized against everything, and that obviously played in his favour; but since when did you have only to wave a medical cer-tificate to be fawned on?

He was bereft and therefore available, but that didn't explain anything either. In that circle, availability was the norm, not the exception. Moreover, he had a reputation for always being absolutely faithful (aside from some escapades at the baths, but that was long ago and didn't really count), which made him an object of curiosity, but that still wasn't much. Do straight men throw themselves at the feet of ugly old widows just because they've always been faithful? Why should it be different for gay men? No, you had to look elsewhere, and that elsewhere probably had something to do with Réjean. A good-looking hunk, Réjean. *He'd* never had to drape himself in chains and leather to look virile. And hung....

What can he possibly be doing with Donald? people must have wondered in the bars, beds, and baths of the village. The question had most likely changed gradually over the years: *What is it Donald does for him?* And since imagination abhors a vacuum....

Réjean hadn't left him a cent, but he had bequeathed him the finest reputation you could imagine; rumour had transformed Donald into a sexual animal, the possessor of unmentionable secrets and mysterious powers.

His role of tearful lover, faithful even beyond the grave, was getting harder and harder to keep up, especially when he came to sit in this bar where the waiters would have killed each other for the privilege of serving him. Though his usual table was nowhere near the stage, that didn't stop the dancers from putting on their show just for him. Even the cooks got into it; when they weren't decorating his plate suggestively, they were slipping messages into his pastry.

So why should he condemn himself to eat all alone in his empty apartment? Wasn't it his turn to be served now, after spending the last six months of his life spoon-feeding Réjean? Fair was fair, after all, and not the least of his pleasures was being offered a cognac after dinner, and sipping it slowly, to the health of Réjean.

None of this would last, of course. One more reason to enjoy it now. In fact, his star was already beginning to fade when Alex became a habitué of the place.

He too had his own table, his own attentive courtiers, which in his case at least seemed justified. You didn't often see such a young man here, unless he was a professional. But from what Donald had been told, Alex refused all advances and actually looked scandalized if anyone offered him money. He was waiting for the right man, he said to anyone who would listen, and that helped to feed the wildest, most incredible rumour heard in the village for years: not only was Alex young and handsome, he was still a virgin.

§

No one on the staff or among the regulars was really surprised when Alex finally decided to get up when he'd finished eating and slowly, confidently, walk over to the table where Donald had barely finished his cognac; stars are destined to meet and merge into one another.

Such a silence fell over the room that even the dancer stopped. Had it not been for the thumping reggae music that no one thought to turn off, they might have heard what was said. Alex and Donald exchanged only a few shy remarks, apparently, and several witnesses would have sworn that they both blushed.

Although the two left a few minutes apart, their little game didn't fool anyone.

The dancer resumed his act, without much conviction, for an audience whose minds were occupied elsewhere.

CHAPTER 21

Families are unadventurous; they only go out on sunny Sunday afternoons. Since the weatherman had mentioned a chance of rain and northerly winds, the bike paths would be empty; they could travel along the Richelieu River at their own speed all the way to the American border. And then.... Alex didn't have to say another word; Guillaume accepted his proposal enthusiastically.

They set out early Tuesday morning and pedalled quickly to Chambly, where they got onto the bike path, which was, as they'd expected, nearly deserted. They raced twenty kilometres before catching their breath by riding more slowly, side by side. As they hadn't seen each other since the incidents that had marked the beginning of summer, they had a great deal to talk about, and they rode along like that for over an hour, so slowly that they were holding up traffic.

Alex talked about Raphaël, about Francis, Stéphanie, and many other things, before finally turning to the topic that had prompted him to call Guillaume. But still he hesitated before getting to the point; what would happen if his friend insisted that he reveal his source? And wasn't that what he was hoping for, deep down?

He beat about the bush by alluding to a family reunion (which wasn't really a lie, as long as the terms weren't defined) where he'd run into a long-lost uncle, an old uncle who worked for a dry cleaner....

"You heard something about Geneviève?"

Guillaume, who so far had been listening absent-mindedly while he wondered what Alex was getting at, was suddenly all ears, very interested in hearing the rest. It hardly mattered to him that there wasn't a restaurant or even a park bench near where he'd applied the brakes. Alex had word of Geneviève, and that wasn't something they could talk about while pedalling, even slowly. They had to sit down — over there, on the other side of the ditch, between the bulrushes and the fence. Ten seconds were all it took him to find a suitable spot, sit on his helmet, and offer Alex his bottle of lukewarm water.

"Well?"

Couldn't you wait till I finished drinking? thought Alex.

He too sat on his helmet, and he repeated everything he'd found out: Geneviève, who didn't know a thing about business, had bought a dry-cleaner's shop that was headed for bankruptcy; she'd got it back on its feet in record time, and there was already a real possibility that it would show a profit. According to what he'd found out from his *very privileged* source, Geneviève had shown exceptional acumen in turning to this neglected sector. Now that she'd acquired some experience and transformed her innate business sense into something more profound, more *philosophical* (yes, that was the word Donald used), perhaps she wouldn't stop there. Who knew if they wouldn't soon see her running a chain of dry-cleaners; maybe she'd use it as a springboard to buy something else.... "It's funny though, isn't it?"

"What?"

"You've been in business school for three years now, you're going to Harvard for an MA and maybe a doctorate. And meanwhile, Geneviève buys a dry-cleaner's. Which is one way to get started in business. It's as if she wants to show you something, even though..."

"Even though what?"

Alex wished he hadn't brought up something he'd have preferred to introduce later, delicately — or not at all. To judge by Guillaume's reaction, he'd better complete his remark as quickly as possible, if he didn't want to be battered to death with a bicycle pump.

"Okay — according to...to my source, Geneviève's tied up with a cop."

"She's been arrested?"

"No. They're involved. I though you'd want to know."

Guillaume sat there in silence for a moment, long enough to thoroughly take in what he'd just heard; then he jumped on his bike without a word, and started pedalling so fast that Alex had trouble following him.

As he pedalled, Guillaume thought of the thousands of movies and novels in which, after a mad race against the clock, the hero smashes the window of the church just as his lady love is about to give herself to some rich, ugly old man. Sure, they were just stories, but such things must have happened at least once in human history, mustn't they? And was there anything more disgusting than a cop? She preferred a cop to him!

Alex tried to keep up with his friend's diabolical pace, but he quickly decided to quit. He pedalled home slowly, a little annoyed that Guillaume hadn't even thanked him, and very disappointed that he hadn't asked a single question about this old uncle who knew so much. Had he opened that door just a crack, Alex would have confessed that the man in question held Geneviève in the highest esteem, which was a little surprising in view of his...his natural propensity, let's say, because such things are natural, there's no need to make a fuss over it, and to tell the truth, this man isn't his uncle or even a near relation, but he's someone very close all the same.... Ask me some questions, Guillaume, please ask me some questions....

He could have come out with it, true, but it was too late now, and that was too bad; he'd probably never again have such a fine opportunity to confide such an intimate secret to a friend; and best of all, the friend in question wouldn't have heard a thing.

§

Guillaume had never travelled the bike path so quickly or complained so much about the loving couples who travelled side by side as if nobody else existed. He didn't slow down when he drove off the path until, trying to make it through an amber light, he was nearly run down by a bus. Then his heart protested so violently that he had to stop by the roadside for a while.

After that, he got back on the road, pedalling more slowly now, which gave him time to wonder if he really felt like smashing a church window.

Stéphanie was the kind of girl who seemed destined to be an excellent second choice, who had always known this, and was perfectly happy about it, as Francis had said. That view was all the more cruel because it was accurate.

Yes, Stéphanie was a second choice, there was no getting around it. But she was also — and the qualification was important — an *excellent* second choice. A cheerful, uncomplicated girl who knew where she was going. Obstacles? What obstacles? Why should there be obstacles if you decided there weren't any? She only had to think about the future and it would match her desires, and nothing would stop her from getting a degree from Harvard and landing a job with a major bank that would send her out to set up branches across Latin America.... A girl who wanted to win, that was what she was, with no complexes, and absolutely no thirst for revenge. A girl who simply wanted to make the most of her abilities, because that suited her — just fine. And who told you all that in her big bed that smelled so good, while she held out one of those little joints she rolled so expertly; you took a hit while she was choking on a burst of laughter, and that might be the most wonderful thing of all, the way her laugh still went on when you caressed her. All right, so what came next was a little cold, more like aerobic exercise than a sacred experience, but what were sacred experiences about? About living as well as you could, and that was all, right?

And maybe he'd end up really falling in love with her. After being in love without knowing it, being in love by default, and being in love after the fact, wasn't he entitled, for once, to be in love in advance? And hadn't he nearly got into a fight over her? That was something, after all. Wasn't it?

Why should he smash a church window for a girl who would never be more than the owner of a chain of dry-cleaners, at the very most? Think about it: cleaning other people's dirty clothes! And to marry a cop, the ultimate degradation!

A chain of dry-cleaners paid for and financed by her father, that was the only possible explanation. Her father, who could never stand him, who had lied like a cheap dentist and had schemed to oust him. Yes, to oust him; if there's one lesson to be gained from this sad story, it was to watch out for the fathers of girlfriends, especially if they were lawyers. There's nothing more treacherous than a man who refuses to get old, who thinks of his daughter as his most precious possession, and who can't stand competition. Maybe Bernard Vallières would be more tolerant of the cop, some dumb guy who wouldn't get under his skin.

Guillaume had locked his bike to a fence near Stéphanie's car, but he came back before he'd taken two steps, just to check that the U-lock was bolted. After that, he stuffed the key in his pocket but took it out again right away; maybe he'd broken the mechanism by double-locking it?

He knew perfectly well what would happen next: he'd travel aimlessly through the city streets, on the pretext that he was thinking things over, till he found himself in Geneviève's neighbourhood. He could fake a blowout just outside her place; then he'd go inside to see his Geneviève dressed up as a cleaner of clothing, Geneviève and her cop, and it would serve no other purpose than to make him hurt even more.

He inserted the key in the lock but he couldn't turn it. Instead, he switched his attention to the valves, unscrewing the caps; he deflated the tires and took a deep breath of the polluted, deliciously acrid air that came out of them. Now he was ready to go. All he had to do was hoist the bike onto the rack on the back of Stéphanie's car. It was over.

Chapter 22

As long as they stick to the role of customers, humans respond to motivations so simple they can be taught in universities. For instance, it takes just a few rainy days at the approach of autumn for people to renew their acquaintance with their favourite dry-cleaners. The cleaners' competence, their attitude towards the clientele, the general appearance of the store, and the prices they charge obviously play a part in their success, but that's not the main thing. The main thing is the customer's hope that his clothes will come back brightened up, and the cleaners' need to earn their living. So the customer turns in his soiled clothing for a shiny new piece of cardboard, and a few days later exchanges the same piece of cardboard, now creased, for his clean clothes. He pays the amount agreed upon, the cleaner hands him a receipt, and that's all there is to it.

It sometimes happens that the human being inside the customer spills over a little; then the customer feels pressed to express his frustration or indulge in confidences or try out his powers of seduction. A bit of experience and dexterity are generally all it takes to convince him that it's to everyone's advantage to keep life simple. The customer goes back to being a customer, the proprietor a proprietor, and all is well.

Obviously our relationships with employees, colleagues,

or business partners are more complex, but even there it's to everyone's advantage never to exceed the boundaries laid down by our roles.

Now, those are excellent principles, but unfortunately they're no help at all if you want to complicate your life rather than simplify it.

Geneviève didn't want to turn Brodeur into a second Donald; pleasant as that relationship was, it was missing a little something that would have made it completely satisfying. All Geneviève asked was to let her heart be won over, even if she no longer knew how to behave in such circumstances (then again, had she ever known?)

She wanted to wait for his phone call, to wait and nothing more, even if it meant being subjected to Donald's roguish smile whenever the phone made her jump. She wanted to think that, far from being prompted only by their own selfish interests, her customers showed the purest self-abnegation in giving her something to keep her busy so time would pass more quickly while she waited to see Brodeur again.

She wanted to be with him one more time, and then a third. After that they'd get married. For ever. Because these things were so complicated that no one should have to live through them twice.

And she wanted Brodeur not to be a policeman — at least, not with her.

Maybe she should just tell him the unvarnished truth and then never bring it up again. I'm the one who did it, Lieutenant Brodeur. That bank in the Laurentians. The dynamite, the vault. It was me. Acting alone. You have no witnesses or evidence, you'll never be able to convict me, but I want you to know. I don't intend to start again, so I'm no danger to society, and I have no regrets. If I'd known what was going to happen afterwards, I'd have done it ages ago; I'd have spared myself six months of Le Pussy. All I know, and even that only a little, is that I like my work, I don't want to lose it, and I still want to slow down — but not alone. That's why I'll never tell anyone else what I've just told you, especially not a judge. You have no proof or witness and you never will. I can invent an alibi, hire a good lawyer, buy off the members of the jury, undress in front of the judge if I have to (it wouldn't be the first time), but I will not confess. The question is whether you can live with that, Lieutenant Brodeur. Because I can.

And that was what she would tell him at the first opportunity. It would be as sharp and straightforward as the crease in a pair of pants.

§

Brodeur phoned on Tuesday morning, on the stroke of ten. Again he'd let three days go by before contacting her. And again he had trimmed an hour off the prescribed waiting period, which was a good sign. Geneviève was grateful; she couldn't stand to wait any longer.

First he asked, his tone strangely formal, if she would see him again the following Saturday — it being understood that this would constitute their second official meeting — and whether she had any objections to his being the one, this time, who suggested the activities that would occupy them for several hours; said activities, which he'd already planned, would not embarrass a well-brought-up young lady, said young lady would be back home by whatever time suited her, and his intentions were entirely honourable.

Geneviève liked the ceremonious tone in which he wrapped the firmness of his remarks. She wouldn't have wanted someone spineless. And he had lots of breath, for a smoker. She also appreciated his saying that his intentions were entirely honourable. It sounded starchy and old-fashioned but at the same time wonderfully perverse; for didn't it suggest that they could be otherwise?

She spent the balance of the week going over the rest of the conversation to herself, in search of clues: she wouldn't need special clothing or a large sum of money or anything else; he would pick her up on the stroke of one p.m., and perhaps she could be waiting on the sidewalk so he wouldn't have to honk his horn.

So he was planning to use his car. Very good. But then what? He'd probably come up with something more original than going back to the Laurentians. A movie? It wasn't the ideal place for getting to know each other, but still, it could have a certain charm: an empty theatre on a Saturday afternoon, his hand on hers....

And then he'd probably invite her to dinner at a restaurant, which would be as banal as it was disappointing. A man has to be singularly lacking in self-confidence, or very old, to take a young woman he barely knows to a restaurant. Unless of course he's trying to impress her with his wallet, which is even worse.

The zoo, a concert, a museum, the planetarium? A walk on Mount Royal? A bar with nude dancers? Hadn't he let a hint of irony peep through when he declared that he wouldn't suggest anything that would embarrass a well-bred young woman? After the striptease she'd made him submit to, it would be just deserts.

Geneviève ran through a number of possibilities, from unlikely to utterly far-fetched, and it wasn't till Saturday morning that she thought of the most unpleasant one of all: what if Brodeur took her to a police station, sat at his typewriter with a cigarette stuck in his mouth, and shone a lamp in her face? Let's begin at the beginning, Mademoiselle Vallières: family name, Christian name, address, marital status....

All things considered, maybe she should wait a little longer before telling him the unvarnished truth.

§

Brodeur drove along the side streets of an anonymous suburb on the South Shore, so slowly you'd have thought he was looking for a house for sale. He finally stopped his car on a crescent much like thousands of other streets, except that it was in this neighbourhood, nowhere else, that he'd spent his childhood. He showed her his parents' house, his playground, his school, and his church, telling her a few anecdotes that were by no means original and, for that very reason, were worth listening to.

He talked about his father, who had worked all his life as a simple labourer and had turned down the foreman's position every time it was offered. The boss could buy his muscles, he used to say, but not his spirit. You can always whistle while you're building furniture, but it's hard when you're adding up columns of figures, and even harder when you're in charge of other men.

His mother had been scandalized when she heard him talk like that; she had plenty of ambition, vicariously at least. When she realized that she'd never achieve anything through her husband, she fell back on her children, who nearly all had university degrees.

Maybe one day he would introduce her to his mother, Brodeur said as he got back in the car. She'd certainly be glad to know that her son was going out with the daughter of a big lawyer. And maybe Geneviève would meet his brother and sisters too, but there was no rush.

Then he talked about Suzanne. It had taken him quite a while to realize that his ex was a little too much like his mother. She'd have liked him to go on taking courses, climbing rungs, filling in squares on a calendar. As for him, he didn't want to move so fast. He liked his job in spite of all the paperwork; he felt he was helping people, and having problems to solve was intellectually stimulating. He didn't feel like changing his life — his professional life, he hastened to add. Which didn't escape Geneviève, who felt herself shiver.

"Another thing I like is visiting houses when I'm on a case. Sometimes you can just open a door and right away you get a sense of boredom, or tragedy, or quiet happiness....

You also find out a lot more about people than you do by talking to them for hours.... Shall we go to my place? My intentions are entirely honourable, of course."

"And then we'll go to my place, I suppose?"

"That's what I had in mind, yes."

"Isn't that called a search in your profession?"

"If that's what you think, maybe we should go there right away."

"All right, let's get it over with."

§

The drive seemed to take an eternity. Sitting side by side in the car, what they resembled was not so much an old couple with nothing left to say to one another, as a couple in the midst of a divorce: they had so much to talk about, and so little chance of making themselves understood, that they preferred to keep quiet.

§

"A souvenir," she explained when Brodeur picked up the plaster donkey. Those words had trouble making their way out, but the rest tumbled forth quickly. The time had come, no matter how it all happened:

"My former colleagues at Le Pussy had a weird sense of humour. Maybe I'll tell you about it some day. And before you start playing Sherlock Holmes, I'd like to point out that the ashtray collection belonged to Réjean, the former owner. I offered them to Donald but he didn't want them. He can't stand incense any more. I burn it sometimes, but if I were you I wouldn't follow that trail; money has no odour. You can even use it in the refrigerator, it works better than baking soda."

"Have you tried that?"

"Could be. Why not check?"

"Do you really want me to?"

"At the rate you're going...."

Brodeur gently set the plaster donkey down beside the ox, but he didn't dare go to the kitchen. Nor did he dare turn towards Geneviève, or even go on exploring the bookcase.

Had he been a Japanese suitor, Brodeur could have asked permission to look through her photo album. He could have immersed himself in Geneviève's childhood and learned all there was to know about her schools, her holidays, her parents, and her friends. But he didn't even let himself take the album off its shelf; he wouldn't have been able to stop himself from looking for clues.

The Japanese suitor would also have taken a look at the books, especially the novels. A few titles would have taught him his fiancée's tastes as well as her notion of love. But the cop would have shaken the books in the hope of seeing money come drifting out.

And so Brodeur stood rooted there in front of the plaster figurines. He felt squeezed in between the eyes of the animals in the crèche — as stupid as they were pointless now, in August — and the eyes of Geneviève, which he could feel glued to his back. He need only turn to her to see which one would carry the day: the cop or the Japanese suitor.

She would be sitting like a queen in her wicker armchair, legs tucked away chastely. He would look at her white blouse buttoned to the neck, he'd allow himself to fall under the spell of her Asian smile, and he'd lay down his arms, his doubts, and his fragmentary evidence at her feet. In fact, that was what he should have done, instead of standing there like a moron, gawking at an ox and ass that didn't even have a baby Jesus to warm up.

Coiled around herself, arms crossed as if to stop herself from biting her nails, Geneviève looked not like a queen but like a little girl caught misbehaving.

"There's some in the freezer and some in a cardboard carton at the back of the closet."

She spoke in an undertone, her eyes fixed on an invisible point on the bare floor. Brodeur moved carefully to the other chair, and sat in it without making a sound. He too stared at the floor.

"If I were a policeman," he said at length, "I wouldn't search your belongings. I don't have a warrant. And there wouldn't be any point anyway; you're entitled to be wary of the banks. If I were a policeman, I'd be sitting here across from you, and I'd be looking into your eyes. Yes, that's the first thing I'd do. Look into your eyes."

Geneviève ventured a glance at Brodeur; while he was saying the words, he never took his eyes off the invisible spot.

"I'd look into your eyes," he repeated again — as if, having sensed her gaze, he wanted to confirm that he knew perfectly well what he was doing. "And no, I wouldn't ask a lot of questions. I'd talk to you about the night of December 19th, about the red wig, the dynamite. I'd point out some contradictions, casually, as if I weren't going to touch them. I'd pretend I had all the evidence I needed, and I might even try a little bluffing by making you think I had witnesses. I'd speak very slowly, with long pauses between my sentences, and I'd observe your slightest reactions. I'd behave as if I knew all I needed, as if the case were closed. I wouldn't accuse you. No, I'd be your friend who understands you and wants to help you unburden yourself. I would play my part so well that you'd end up believing me. You'd give me a neat little confession and I'd listen to you like a friend, without interrupting. You'd end up confessing, I'm sure of it. You'd feel so good, so relieved...."

"And what about you? How would you feel?"

"Glad I'd manipulated you so well, obviously, but I wouldn't show it. I would listen to you attentively, and then I'd probably think about the report I had to write for my superiors, about my chance of promotion.... If I were just a cop, that's what I'd do."

"And what if I told you that you didn't need a search

warrant or any psychological tricks?"

"Are we still speaking in the conditional?"

"Yes, of course."

"I'd tell you that I'm not just a cop, and that you could tell me whatever you wanted, on one condition: you had to wait another few weeks. In the meantime we could talk about something else. By the way, are you allergic to cats?"

"What would be different in a few weeks?"

"A detail, one very small detail, but for me it's a question of conscience. It's in the Criminal Code. Section twenty-three, part one: 'An accessory after the fact to an offence is one who, knowing that a person has been a party to the offence, receives, comforts, or assists him for the purpose of enabling him to escape.'"

"You know the code by heart?"

"Only the parts I'm interested in. And what I'm interested in right now is section twenty-three. I've read it dozens of times, trying to put myself in a lawyer's shoes. We could talk for hours about the exact meaning of the word 'knowing,' of course, but that's not too important. What I'm interested in is part two. Are you familiar with it?"

"No, why should I be?"

"I don't know. Your father's a lawyer..."

"Is that a policeman's trick, looking into my eyes like that?"

"Yes. It's still the best lie-detector around. Look me in the eye and swear to me that you don't know part two of section twenty-three of the Criminal Code."

"No, I don't know it. I swear I don't."

"I'm very glad. Let me quote: 'No married person whose spouse has been a party to an offence is an accessory after the fact to that offence by receiving, comforting or assisting the spouse for the purpose of enabling the spouse to escape.' You understand why I'd be disappointed if you told me you were familiar with that part."

After a long reflection, Geneviève's reply was simply "No."

"No what?"
"No, I'm not allergic to cats."

CHAPTER 23

As usual, the room is very small and very warm. There's no straight chair or easy chair, not even a cushion, and the client has to sit on the floor, on a piece of matting. While he waits for the show to begin, he can always admire the decor: a reproduction of a Chinese painting (a banal landscape drawn on a square of fabric hanging from a strip of bamboo, with quantities of dangling gold fringe), a transparent tissue-paper screen in the same style, and a large fan fastened to the wall above the roll of paper towels and the fire extinguisher. The Orient in all its splendour, the Bill Wong version. To add to the ambience, there's twangy music that gets on your nerves, but it has the advantage of covering the knuckle-cracking of the bouncer waiting in the corridor. You'd like to run away, but you stay put. You have to.

And then she walks in. Her name, apparently, is Tao. Very long glossy black hair and slanted eyes, as you might expect. Chinese, Cambodian, Vietnamese — that part of the world. Impossible to nail down her nationality, even less her age. Early twenties, let's say. Tao is wearing a hideous fluorescent green kimono with big fuchsia-coloured flowers. It's very ugly, but who cares? You want to look into Tao's eyes, that's all. You aren't asking her to believe, just to pretend she does. You'd like a wink, a smile to show that it's just a game, that there's nothing to get worked up about. You're two consenting adults who've made a deal, that's all: fifty dollars for a simulated smile, if you please, Ms. Tao.

Tao doesn't take her kimono off right away, but one by one she removes the chopsticks holding up her long hair; it's a wig, of course, but no sooner has the thought of a wig crossed your mind than you've forgotten it; you don't want to know. It's at that precise moment, when you've decided you don't want to know, that you start to believe; you believe in this as you do in everything else, because it's what you're looking for, or because you've paid, it doesn't matter, you just have to want to believe and then stop thinking. So you watch Tao take down her long hair and then go behind the screen, where she switches on a little spotlight that will cast silhouettes; finally she sheds her kimono, crouches by a stream — at least, that's what's suggested by the music, recorded over a background of birdsong and lapping waves — and splashes her face. Her hands travel down her body; you look at her and you believe it, yes, because the sooner you believe, the sooner it's under way.

Then you go home and try to describe it all to Monique, who isn't interested. "Look, Bernard, you don't have to give me the details, I know what goes on." You insist on explaining to her once again that you didn't go to Le Pussy as a turn-on, regardless of what she thinks, but she only shrugs. You follow her from room to room, telling her how important images are to the male imagination — she ought to be interested in such a revelation — but with no more success; your wife, whose business it is to listen, doesn't want to listen to you. You feel slightly wounded, but you don't hold it against her. Your own thoughts on the matter are not advanced enough yet to be presented convincingly, and she'd reproach you, quite rightly, for your bad faith.

You think about Tao again at night, in the conjugal bed, after Monique is asleep, and you take up your story where you left off. Tao seems not to understand a single word of

French or English, and her only response is "Hee-hee" or a bow. You ask your questions anyway, without much conviction; you've paid for your thirty minutes, you may as well take advantage of them.

"Do you know a young woman gymnast, *jeune femme gymnaste, un deux trois*, with barbells...?"

"Hee-hee," responds Tao, with more bows.

"Her name was Roxane, I think."

"Roxane go away, hee-hee."

You have the nasty impression that she's laughing at you outright, but so what? The others weren't very chatty either. Those girls stick together, and you can't really blame them.

Still, there was a gymnast who called herself Roxane, that much is established, and this Roxane may very well have been Geneviève. She started working last August — just after she dumped Guillaume — and held out for six months, long enough to amass a little capital. And then things get complicated; where does Brodeur come in? A policeman suddenly appears in the picture and she introduces him as her fiancé. A fiancé she's just met and she's rushing off to marry, as if there were nothing more urgent. In our day we'd have counted the months while we kept an eye on her belly, but in this day and age, for heaven's sake, why should a young couple be in such a hurry? Geneviève, who may have worked at Le Pussy; Brodeur, who's a cop....

"Well?" says Monique, whenever you reach that point in your reflections.

"Well, doesn't it bother you, knowing that your daughter..."

"Bernard, listen to me: Geneviève owns a dry-cleaner's shop. And like it or not, we have to resign ourselves to that. She wants to marry a policeman. That's her business. Why invent problems for her instead of solving your own?"

"I've got problems?"

"That's what I've been telling you, over and over, from

the outset: you're obsessed with your daughter, so you have a hard time accepting that she has a normal sex life. Instead of feeling guilty or denying the problem or rationalizing, the way most parents do, you project — you fantasize."

"I fantasize?"

"You certainly do. And that gives you a perfect opportunity to satisfy your fantasies."

"Listen, Monique, I've explained a hundred times..."

"I know. You make such a cute jealous father.... Good night, Bernard."

"Good night," you reply, before you turn over and grumble: so I've fantasized the whole thing, have I? And Guillaume, was he fantasizing too, when he told you that business about a client at Pro-Gym who offered Geneviève fifty dollars an hour to wriggle around in a cubicle?

And the owner of Pro-Gym, who was so afraid of lawyers that he let you look over his client list, did you make him up too? And was it *by chance* that one of those clients also owned a twenty percent share in Le Pussy, where all your dreams become reality and personal cheques are accepted?

Geneviève works at Le Pussy for six months and quits her job shortly after Christmas. She has enough to pay her rent and maybe she's even accumulated a little capital which she invests in her dry-cleaning shop. It stands up pretty well, for a fantasy.

But all right, since it seems I'm the only one interested.... Two a.m. already. What's Geneviève cooking up with her policeman? Maybe she has insomnia too, maybe she's staring at the ceiling or at the green light from her clock-radio; maybe she isn't sleeping because he snores — he must be the kind who snores, yes, but he's a good guy anyway, her Brodeur. Looks strong, too. He'll be able to protect her. And hold her hand, on days when the wind is strong.

That's what you have to tell yourself, I imagine.